PRAISE FOR LAUREN DANE AND HER NOVELS

Praise for MESMERIZED

"Wow! What a sexy and fun read. Dane has a way of making the futures seem so real and believable with characters that just pop off the page. Love it!"
—*Fresh Fiction*

"From the first chapter, *Mesmerized* grabs you by the throat and leads you through an exciting twist of sensuous romantic and science fiction adventure... A well-told blend of hot sensual romance and science fiction."
—*Night Owl Reviews*

"No one combines space opera and erotica quite like Dane. If you thought the only thing missing from Joss Whedon's Firefly series was a little explicit sex, you have to check out *Mesmerized*."
—*RT Book Reviews*, 4 1/2 stars

Praise for INSATIABLE

"The story line is fast-paced and loaded with action as the irresistible force meets the unmovable object when two enemies from different life stations fall into heated love . . . This is quite a sizzler."
—*Genre Go Round Reviews*

"Dane has created a fully realized, intricate world with thoughtful, sympathetic characters, which makes it easy to lose oneself in the romance . . . The cliffhanger ending will leave readers panting for the next installment."
—*RT Book Reviews*

"Lauren Dane is one of the best authors out there writing exciting, on-the-edge-of-your-seat science fiction romance . . . *Insatiable* is also a great suspenseful thriller where the chase will leave some readers breathless."
—*Babbling About Books, and More*

"Another awesome entry in Dane's Federation Chronicles."
—*Book Binge*

Praise for RELENTLESS

"In typical Lauren Dane fashion, *Relentless* will sweep you away to a place where passion and romance rule the day . . . Pick up *Relentless* and discover why Dane made my auto-buy list long ago."
—Anya Bast, author of *Jeweled*

"Dane's *Relentless* is exceptional for its realism, because she quite capably articulates a class-based society in an intriguing alternative world. Dane gives us a down-to-earth pairing of decent, appealing individuals who struggle to find peaceable solutions for their people, while hoping for the chance of an enduring love with one another."
—Joey W. Hill, author of *A Vampire's Claim*

"Hot romance, detailed world-building and a plot focusing on righting injustice make *Relentless* a page-turner. With passion and politics, Dane delivers again!"
    —*Megan Hart, author of Tempted*

"Ms. Dane takes readers on a roller-coaster ride of emotions . . . This is a fabulous read for fans of sci-fi with a generous helping of erotic romance. I hope that we'll be seeing more installments in this futuristic world."
    —*Darque Reviews*

"Spectacular . . . absolutely brilliantly written."
    —*Manic Readers,* 4½ stars

"Pulled in from page one, readers will enjoy the delicious sensuality."
    —*RT Book Reviews,* 4½ stars

"Emotionally charged, passionate and at times volatile, *Relentless* once again proves that Ms. Dane is a first-class author who is fully capable of delivering exactly the sorts of story lines that readers crave."
    —*Romance Junkies,* 5 Blue Ribbons

"Filled with heat and erotic passion . . . *Relentless* is a do-not-miss."
    —*Joyfully Reviewed*

"This terrific science fiction erotic romance is fast-paced and filled with action in and out of the bedroom."
    —*Midwest Book Review*

"Fiery, erotic and rich with plot, this book is definitely a keeper on my shelf."
    —*Night Owl Romance*

Praise for UNDERCOVER

"Lauren Dane deftly weaves action, intrigue and emotion with spicy, delicious eroticism. *Undercover* is a toe-curling erotic romance sure to keep you reading late into the night."
　　—Anya Bast, author of *Witch Heart*

"Sexy, pulse-pounding adventure with a heart twist of emotion that'll leave you weak in the knees. Dane delivers!"
　　—Jaci Burton, author of *Riding on Instinct*

"Exciting, emotional and arousing! *Undercover* by Lauren Dane is a ride well worth taking."
　　—Sasha White, author of *My Prerogative*

"Fast-paced action, steamy romance, two sizzling heroes and a heroine—Dane does it again!"
　　—Megan Hart, author of *Tempted*

"Scintillating! Lauren Dane delivers a roller coaster of emotion, intrigue and sensual delights in *Undercover*. I was hooked from the first sentence."
　　—Vivi Anna, author of *Veiled Truth*

"*Undercover* is a compelling and wild read."
　　— *Manic Readers*

"Will garner more than a few new fans for Ms. Dane's work."
　　— *Wild on Books*

"Dane has written a sizzling, delicious tale of love lost, found and expanded . . . As endearing as it is molten hot. The friction between Sera and Ash as they resolve their past is intense, and with Brandt added to the mix, it's nothing short of explosive."
    —*RT Book Reviews*, 4½ stars

"Wow! This book rocks!"
    —*Romance Junkies*

"Hot, sexy and action-packed . . . A fabulous read!"
    —*Fresh Fiction*

LAND'S END

LAUREN DANE

CHAPTER ONE

LOYAL LED the escort up the wide expanse of Highway, up the ramp and the steep roadway. To Silver Cliffs.

To Verity Coleman.

He had a shell in his pocket. One he'd leave for her on the morning they pushed on to the next garrison. He knew the pink insides would delight her. Knew the swirling shape and smooth surface would bring a smile to her lips.

Escorting a transport to Silver Cliffs was his job. The same as he escorted to other garrisons up and down the Highway. But *she* drew him there. Like a magnet. He found himself rushing through his last day any time Silver Cliffs was next on the list.

He was a lawman. He didn't just take official traffic to the garrisons; he brought law and order. He brought the hammer down when necessary. He was the face of a government that could be beneficent, or brutal.

Every day he had to be hard. He *was* a hard man. Had seen a lot. Had done worse. He was a killer when he had to be. Solved disputes along the Highway when they pulled into town. Sometimes that included putting men down for crimes that put the rest of the garrison in danger.

He was good at his job. And for most of his life he'd been happy to do it with no real ties to anyone outside his crew. The men and women he traveled with were also lawmen. Also trained. Under his command they did whatever was necessary and he counted on that over and over. They were the only people he considered himself close to.

One of the escort vehicles at the rear hailed him. "Road is clear behind us. I, for one, am looking forward to some quiet downtime in a room with a bed and none of you anywhere near me and Marcus. A hot meal, a warm bath and a good night's sleep. Heaven."

Trinity, one of his men, and her partner, Marcus, traveled together in their crew. The two of them had a deep and abiding connection. Intense and physical as well. It softened a hard-edged job to have that. Trinity had her own demons to deal with, and since she and Marcus had ended up together, she'd been stronger, steadier.

Being constantly on edge was hard on a body. Their world was hard enough, even for those living in the garrisons. But out there on the road they saw things daily that chipped away at their humanity. Made them jaded and cynical about humanity. Sex was a way to blow off steam. To work out the kinks in your heart as well as your muscles. But he sure as hell didn't need love to get sex.

Sure he liked fucking. A whole hell of a lot. It chased away the brutality from his skin and the taste from his mouth for the time he'd buried himself in a woman. When he felt the physical need to be with a woman, he filled it. There were plenty of women all along the Highway who had no problem laying with a lawman. He'd never needed to pay or barter for it.

He'd been fine with that for years. Until Verity.

After a time on the Southern Highway, he'd been assigned to the northern sector. The first time he laid eyes on her, she'd been standing out at the loading dock where the official transport would unload goods into the back of her mercantile.

Red hair rode in a long, braided rope down her back. She'd been young then. She was young now. Back then she'd been capable, as most were out there on the edge. But she had a hesitance about her too. Her eyes had flicked up, gaze locking with his, a sweet smile on her face, and that had been the moment she'd begun to capture his attention.

He knew he should have kept away from her. She wasn't a woman he'd come to bury his cock and his sins in. She was a woman you couldn't walk away from. The kind of woman a man gave himself to body and soul because she was worth that constancy.

But he found himself asking her if she had a room to let, or if she knew where he and his people could stay while they were in Silver Cliffs.

And that's how he found himself in her guest room. Biting his lip as he fucked his fist every night he was there, wishing it was her.

They'd leave and he'd think of her daily. And when it came time to go to Silver Cliffs again, it was as if he came home. Not to the garrison, but to her.

THE HORNS HERALDING visitors coming over the bridge and approaching the gate brought Verity's attention from her perch on the ladder. Certainly whoever might be arriving was far more interesting than dusting off jars and canisters of dry goods on high shelves.

There'd been a blip about a shipment of goods and mail coming. That had been three days ago so it was still a little early. The herald could be traders from one of the other garrisons. But just in case it was official traffic, it wouldn't do to have messy hair and be covered in dust.

She nipped around the back to brush and rebraid her hair after washing her hands and face. On her way out, she unlocked the large doors at the loading bay behind the store. If it was an official transport, she'd be taking deliveries through there. Best to be prepared as the folks from town would be lining up to see what she was getting.

Being past midday, the sun was high, and though it still wasn't quite past the threat of the last snowfall, the day was clear and warm, a hint at the long, warm season to come.

Verity hoped the seeds she'd ordered would be in the shipment if it was indeed a big delivery. Many of the farmers within the high walls of Silver Cliffs had their own seed stores, but since a lot of folks in town kept kitchen gardens, she put in large orders for seeds at the end of every harvest season, knowing they'd show up after the last of the regular snowstorms as the ground readied for planting.

As she walked down the hill toward the garrison gates, she passed the power station. The river was full of melting snowpack so the generators hummed, recharging the banks of batteries that would keep the lights on even in the coldest part of the annum.

She had some solar collection banks James had bought but never did anything with. Last harvest season she'd paid Byson Carter, one of the local boys, to install them on her roof. Her share of payments to the garrison board had gone down by half. She liked that very much. Keeping her freedom was important. Especially in a town where a woman her age remaining unmarried, even after she'd been widowed, was frowned upon.

She paid that no nevermind. She'd done her time under the thumb of a man who used fists and drink as easily as he took a breath. She had no great desire to hitch herself to another anytime soon.

Though that didn't mean she wouldn't enjoy the company of a certain lawman the few times each annum he rolled into Silver Cliffs with official transports.

They'd allowed a crowd to gather along the walkways to either side of the gate so she figured it had to be friendlies of one sort or another.

Otherwise they'd have sounded an alert and men would be running down the street with rifles, heading to their stations. They all stood, going up on tiptoe to try to get a better glimpse of the outside world, hungry for news of what was going on down the valley, up and down the Land's End Highway.

The guards stood on the walkway above the gate, calling out to whoever was beyond. Verity cursed her impatience. If she'd gone to the front bedroom upstairs she'd have been able to see more.

Bits and pieces of chatter reached her ears. People hoping for mail, some awaiting parts for needed machinery. Verity had a list of goods that'd been on backorder for some time. If it was official transport, she'd have some pretty-smelling soaps she'd traded for some of her preserves with a friend down in Banyon Pass.

And there'd be some time with Loyal. She smiled just thinking about him. Her tall, taciturn lawman.

The large wheels that worked to open the gate began to move and a burst of pleasure shot through her as she caught sight of the lead vehicle, a lawman escort. Another just behind it and then the large official transport followed by another two escort vehicles.

Happiness coursed through her. She waved, being unable to see through the heavily fortified front windows, knowing though that he always drove the lead. Hoping he'd feel at least a whisper of the happiness she did.

The excited tone of the gathered crowd pulled her out of her thoughts about Loyal. She needed to get back to the mercantile to take the delivery. The transport always offloaded its goods and deliveries to her. She handled the dissemination to the garrison's citizens. Well, of everything but munitions, and that was something the lawmen did in private, behind the big steel doors of garrison headquarters.

They'd give her no more than half an hour before townspeople began to mill around. She hustled back up the hill, her mind already on work, as the various vehicles went one way or another.

Tobin, her nephew and her assistant at the mercantile, tipped his cap at her from where he stood on the raised loading porch.

She grabbed a pair of gloves and slid an apron on. "Ready?"

"Indeed I am. I'm under orders from my mother to dibs anything she might like." He rolled his eyes affectionately as he spoke.

"By that she means anything sweet or perhaps shiny." Constance was her big sister. She'd been fortunate to marry a man who adored her, who was a true partner. She was satisfied with her life in Silver Cliffs and sometimes had difficulty understanding Verity's wanderlust.

The transport's back doors slid open and the driver tossed up two large burlap bags. Mail then, which would make everyone happy. She took those to the little locked room she delivered the local and outside mail from. As soon as they got everything off, loaded and inventoried, she'd begin the process of sorting the packages and letters.

They passed crates up. Bolts of fabric. Brown paper sacks holding nails and other household needs. Colorful ribbons tied the opaque bags of the sweets her sister loved so much. Jars and cans of all different types. Tobin took delivery of the grain and seeds. The doctor came through the crowd and signed for a shipment of much-needed basic medication for folks in town.

There'd been thin times. Enough that the knot of fear that always began to tighten when she could begin to see the bottom of the drawers of basic foodstuffs in the mercantile loosened. Yes, they could weather lean times. Mostly. But having enough and a little to spare was a good thing. It kept the town easy and satisfied.

And with the days beginning to lengthen and planting season and the hours upon hours of labor that came with it, satisfied was a far better mood for people than the drawn face of worry.

Once she'd signed for everything, the transport would head over to the lot they used while in town. It was at the outer edge of the business center and the residents of Silver Cliffs would be able to drop off things to have them be delivered all up and down the Highway. Verity handled official mail, but there was a steady barter business between all the garrison towns.

"Tobin, get the news and other periodicals out first. I'm going to start on all the mail. Don't unlock the doors until I say so." She headed up to her apartments above the store to check on the stew she'd started that morning. Extra glad now that she knew she'd have a guest.

The place smelled good, the savory herbs and baby onions she'd found on her walk the day before near the river beginning to rise, accompanying the meat from a plump Muscat she'd been paid with. Muscats were nice and fat this time of the annum as they fed on the snow mice that bred in abundance. Her customer had even plucked and dressed it, saving Verity the less than pleasant job.

Another quick look in the mirror in the room Loyal always rented out when he came to town. When she'd received the blip that a transport would be arriving she'd aired it out, giving all the bedding a wash and leaving them in the sun to dry. Mountain lilies sat in a vase on the dresser, lending a deep red splash of color. Readying it for him.

IN HIS SECTOR there were twenty garrison towns. A few were little more than bends in the road of less than a hundred people. All had their own charms in one way or another. But Silver Cliffs was not only beautiful, sitting up on the cliffs above the Highway, it had several farms, a river full of fish, woods full of game and two waterfalls that powered a mill.

There was a sense of plenty in Silver Cliffs that some other garrisons lacked.

They took care of themselves and each other.

He took a leisurely walk up the hill from the garrison offices, his pack slung over his shoulder. The air was so clean up there.

Where Shelter City had thirty thousand residents—far more than

Silver Cliffs' five thousand—it had more industry, more traffic. More noise to the peaceful quiet in Silver Cliffs.

He'd grown up in the back streets, running games for his father to put food on the table.

He shoved that memory away. It'd be good to stay a night or two in Silver Cliffs before they headed for the last two stops, the northernmost garrisons on the Highway.

It seemed as if half the town was lined up at the mail window and the other half milled around inside the mercantile. He knew there'd be extra staff on to help Verity with the crush. Knew she'd be busy.

But he stood in line to see her at the mail office anyway.

He watched her, smiling here and there, scolding anyone who got impatient or rude, laughing and joking as she worked quickly and efficiently.

Nothing about her was wasted. He liked that. Though she did have an abundance of beauty, he noted she always made an effort to tame it when she was in public. Yearned, he could admit in his secret heart, to see all that flame-colored hair down, wild about her face. Desired to rest his hands at the curves hinting at the waist of her wide-legged trousers or the long skirts she wore on days like this one.

He thought of her often when he was out on the road. Miles of emptiness only broken by the memories of her scent, or the way she sounded when she laughed. Even times when he'd had to face the violence of the brigands she came to his mind. The personification of why he did what he did. To make it possible for Verity to continue on in their world.

She looked up and caught his gaze, her smile brightening. "Lawman, well met!"

He tipped his chin. "Good day, Ms. Coleman. I came to see if you had any lodging available."

"Aye. Your room is ready. If you see any of the others, please inform them the bed and breakfast has three rooms available and the Sorens have beds available out at their farmstead as well. You can go on up when you're ready."

He tipped his head again. "Thank you." He moved out of line and headed around back to the stairs leading to her living quarters. He liked that she trusted him enough to give him free rein in her personal space. Most did, of course. Lawmen occupied a revered part of the culture. The lawmen had served on the front lines against the brigands for generations. The populace understood that, respected that. Having one stay in your home was an honor and why he, a single man, would be allowed to stay here in a widow's home without any raised brows.

Or, if there were any rumblings, they'd be kept quiet. The garrisons needed the lawmen to get delivery of goods from all up and down the Highway. Naturally, they'd all need to be put up when they came to town.

Some garrisons had hotels and other traveler lodging. Usually those closer to the capital city. Most had what Silver Cliffs had, rooms to let in various homes, sometimes beds at the garrison headquarters or police stations.

The others would know, of course, each having their favorite places to lodge. Trinity and Marcus would take one of the rooms at the bed and breakfast as they always stayed together. There was a bar down the other end of town, along with two cafes.

He wouldn't need either, of course. He didn't drink in public when he was on a ride. And Verity's cooking would keep him well satisfied while he was in Silver Cliffs. He'd dine with her. Though she tried, always, to refuse his payment, saying without him, she'd lose business. He knew her store made months' worth of revenue on the days an official transport came in. Knew too, she received a salary from the central governance to distribute the mail and be responsible for dissemination of official communication from them via the blip system she maintained in the office downstairs.

But he paid. As he always did elsewhere, though here it made a difference knowing it helped her.

At the top of the stairs his mouth watered as the scent of her kitchen hit. Herbs, some foul. Freshly baked bread. There was a basket on the nightstand in his room with a note that he should eat and bathe until she finished up downstairs.

Bathing sounded mighty fine, as it happened. They'd been on the road two days, having only briefly stopped just down the Highway in Table Mount to deliver fuel. They'd slept in their vehicles and tents as Table Mount was little more than a way station. They could have all slept in barracks, but Loyal preferred to be outside or in his vehicle instead of the confines of a barracks, weather permitting.

She had running water and a decent-sized tub. He ate a few of the corn patties and drank several glasses of water before he headed into her bathroom to wash the road from his skin.

WHEN SHE'D FINALLY FINISHED with the mail, and knew there'd be another line up in the morning when she opened again, she headed into the store to help there. The first people allowed in were those who'd pre-ordered goods. It kept the traffic manageable that first day of the deliveries.

And, she couldn't lie, it also encouraged people to preorder and put down payments on goods, which kept her credit account healthy. She liked the numbers, liked knowing that should she ever need to up and leave Silver Cliffs, she had the means to do it. Liked knowing she'd be able to get herself on a travel list at some point too.

That didn't mean she had the opportunity, not all the time anyway. But she liked having some options in any case.

The store bustled with business, customers wearing smiles as they took their paper-wrapped bundles from the counter. Her storeroom in the back was still full so she'd spend some time stocking after she closed up as well. But for now, she had plenty to do.

Constance worked alongside Tobin, going through the order cards and settling up accounts. Verity pulled out orders as she caught sight of people coming in. Constance's husband, Emeril, also came in a few minutes later, after he'd left his job down at the credit office for the day. He worked there during the snow season but everyone cut hours back during planting and harvest time. They had a sizable plot of land and grew grain they ground at the mill and sold in town.

The mercantile had belonged to James, but it was *hers* since he'd gone and gotten himself killed three years before. Good riddance to him. And in that time, it not only became hers, but her nephew had come on as her assistant and her sister and brother-in-law helped on delivery days in exchange for goods.

Emeril was wary of her. She knew he didn't like her curiosity. Had made multiple comments to Constance about how she needed to settle down and get married at last instead of flitting around town. But he was there to help and that's what mattered.

She also liked knowing that right above them Loyal stretched out those long legs on the bed in her spare room. Or lounged naked in her tub. As she measured out fabric and cut it, wrapping it up for her customers, she went back to an old favorite fantasy.

One where she'd come upstairs and stand in the doorway to the bathroom. He'd look up, surprised, probably smoking one of his fancy cigars. But she'd put her finger to her lips to hush him up.

Each button at the neck of her blouse would come loose as he watched. Down, more and more of her skin would show and he would not move. He would only continue to watch her with those big pale blue eyes that were nearly the color of a snow sky.

She'd slide the blouse from her arms, letting it fall near the clothes he'd removed earlier.

The steam from the water would allow her to pretend they were somewhere far away. The hot springs in the hills above Silver Cliffs maybe. It didn't matter, only that she'd pull her undergarments up and over her head.

Still smoking, he'd look at her, one corner of his mouth quirking up just a tiny bit.

A few buttons and her skirts would slide to her feet in a pool of fabric, leaving her in naught but her drawers, which she'd shed, standing utterly naked before him.

But she wouldn't be a shy widow. No, she'd unbind her hair, shake it out and his pupils would swallow the color in his eyes. His lips would part and he'd hold a hand out. Urging her to step into the big tub and join him.

She'd take the cigar, maybe even take a long drag, letting the smoke inhabit her body. All while his lips cruised over her body, his hands caressing her.

"My goodness, Verity Coleman, whatever are you daydreaming about?"

Faith Ander patted Verity's hand, tearing her from that fantasy and back into her life at the counter.

She blushed furiously.

"I must admit, Faith, I'm starving. I was thinking about the stew on my stove cooking nice and slow all day."

She laughed and Faith joined her. "I imagine on delivery days you don't get much time to have two thoughts in a row much less luncheon."

Verity wrapped the cheerful yellow fabric up and grabbed the blue after she looked at the sheet Faith had brought along. Faith was a seamstress. In fact her clothes were sold in the mercantile all through the year.

"I am fair excited to see what you'll be making with this blue. So pretty."

"Have some skirts and dresses on order for the yellow. Thought the blue would compliment. I haven't forgotten you either, Verity." She patted the green already wrapped and ready to go. "This is for a skirt for you. I think the blue would make a pretty harvest season dress too."

"Yes. Please."

She chitchatted with more people, measured out dry goods and such until at last, long after the sun had begun to fall below the mountains beyond, they finally flipped the sign to *Closed* and she sent everyone home.

CHAPTER TWO

HE SAT in her living room, reading a book. Deep concentration on his face, yet his body was relaxed. It pleased her that he felt safe to do so in her home. Pleased her to have him there.

"Evening, Loyal. I'll be with you shortly and we'll have dinner. Unless you've already eaten?"

He stood and nodded, tipping his chin with respect in a very old-school way. "Evening, Verity. I will admit I ate the entire basket of baked goods you left for me. But I'm more than ready to enjoy that stew. Tempting me all afternoon with that scent."

She smiled. "Thank you. I've spent some time during the last hour or two just thinking about it. I need to wash the day off and I'll return. If you peek in my pantry, you'll find some ale and a bottle of wine. A trader from Charity Bay, he was. Always pays that way."

"I'll get us a glass while you clean up." He nodded at her as she left the room.

She chose a deep blue dress. Casual of course, the type worn in the evenings at home by many women. But the color complimented her skin and hair and she liked looking pretty for him.

In the bathroom she noted he'd left her a gift. He often did that when he stayed with her. Several small soaps shaped like shells. She picked one up and brought it to her nose. The scent was fine, as delicate as the shape. And more, these oval-shaped cakes of every day soap. Though these too had a lovely scent. River lilies, mountain violets and the lush, nearly velvet scent of orchidium, found far south of Silver Cliffs. Past the capital city.

She picked that one and soaped up a washcloth, choosing a quick lather-up instead of a long, leisurely bath. She wanted to be with him, to soak up as much time with him as she could before he left. Once he did, she'd have plenty of time for long baths. Alone.

Brushing out her hair, she spritzed it to keep the curls behaving and chose to bind it loosely so it hung on one shoulder.

Which had been the right choice as he paused, his lips parting slightly when she came back out.

"How's the wine?"

"I saved the first sip until we'd toasted." He handed her a glass and clicked his with it.

"Go dte tu slan." In the old tongue for *safe travels*.

She smiled and repeated it back before taking a sip.

"Sit down and I'll get some bowls filled. There's fresh-churned butter in the cooler."

"Some days, usually while I'm in Silver Cliffs, I wonder if being paid in credits doesn't rob a man of the finer things like cream, honey, fresh butter and the like." He lifted his glass. "Fine wines on a cool evening as well."

"Ah well, I'm sure in the capital you can buy all those things and more with credits."

She ladled up the stew in two large bowls and placed them on the table, returning to her cooler to grab a jar of pickled vegetables.

"Nothing in the capital tastes anything near this good and fresh.

Though I'm of a mind to bring some butter I favor the next time I come. It's caked with salt from the Great Sea. I think you'd like it."

Once she'd settled, he sat, placing the linen napkin across his lap.

"And how do you do, Loyal?"

The stew filled him, warm and delicious. She would have made a good wife. Though from the bits and pieces he knew, the man she'd had before didn't deserve her. Not so very uncommon.

"I do just fine, Verity. And you?"

"The same. My sister is with child again. The rumors, and I know how much you love those"—he snorted at the tease—"are that the garrison chief is sneaking through Madeline Johnston's back door most nights. Course, they're both of age, neither is married to anyone else. He's fine looking, which I suppose is part of it. The jealousy, I mean. The river is full of sweet, fat silver fish. There will be plenty drying all around town this week. You'll be of a knowing when the wind shifts. Planting will begin soon. The ground is softening up. You only just missed the mud." She sighed. "Takes too much time to deal with the floors downstairs when we get a few days of mud. Like all of my life is about sweeping and mopping and sweeping some more. Telling people to kick their shoes a bit afore they come in."

He knew she was hungry for details of the world outside the walls. So when she finished, he'd give them to her. Part of his pleasure in visiting her was sharing those details, watching the delight on her face, hearing the rushed pleasure in the way she asked for more.

"This is a delicious stew. The pickle as well. Did you make it?"

"Yes, thank you. My garden was heavy last season. Had so much extra it seemed a shame to not pickle and put some by. Sold quite a bit downstairs to folks my mother would have termed the grasshoppers, aye?"

He smiled at the memory of the story of the ant and the grasshopper. The ants worked hard to prepare for lean times but the grasshopper lazed about and was caught unawares when the snow fell.

"If she were still alive she'd laugh to know those grasshoppers keep food on my table all snow long."

"Indeed." He shifted in his chair, settling in to speak. "The grass is very tall now down in Solace. They had their thaw two moons back."

"More temperate to the south, yes?" She leaned in, eyes alight as he started to give her those details he knew she wanted.

"Yes, doesn't snow much south of Shelter City. Only round the annum end. Powerful hot in the mid year down there though. No icy cold river to dip your toes in. Though in Solace there's a mighty large lake. In the mid year the town guards it often so folks can go on down after the workday is over, or on off days to cool off."

"Solace has those little cookies?"

"Yes, they're green because the flour they're made with is cut with the sweet grain that grows with the grasses. Seem to recall you have a powerful like for them."

She blushed. "You brought me some last annum. They were delightful with tea."

He'd remembered of course and would leave her a small bundle of them to find once he'd gone.

"And how is the Highway? Jackson down the garrison heard tell the brigands were active again on the southern passes?"

"Unfortunately, yes. Whole town was attacked, Brilliance. One of the furthest south, where the Highway begins."

Her hand went to her chest. "How did the people fare?"

"Many didn't." Including several lawmen who'd been nearby and had raced to help.

She shook her head. "A tragedy to be sure. I'm sure you heard when you checked in that we had some news of scouts."

He had and it had filled him with rage. And worry for her.

"You know if they come you're to head to your storeroom and lock yourself in."

She waved it away. "I know that's what everyone tells me to do. As if

I would hide away when I could help. I'm a good shot with a rifle. I have extra ammunition here. If they come to our gates I will not hide while they burn us to the ground. I will protect my home. But the sentry towers are on alert. We're fine. I have a tunnel, from the cellar out to a plot of land a bit away. I've got food and water, supplies and the like, stored back there too. But I'm staying as long as I can."

He frowned. "Finer if you'd keep yourself safe instead of trying to do battle with scum like the brigands. They won't just burn things, if you take my meaning. Beautiful woman like you has far more to worry over."

"If you think women are unaware of such dangers, you have no idea what it's like to live in this world as a woman." She pursed her lips and sniffed as she delivered her set to and he had to grip his spoon to keep from touching her as the heat of want washed over him.

Prim and proper Verity was delightful enough, but when she got fire in her eyes? His cock grew hard and heavy and his mouth watered to take a taste of her lips. And other parts.

"I appreciate the way women are viewed." He nodded. "But I know these brigands. They would rip everything you hold dear to shreds."

He spent the rest of the meal entertaining her with stories about all the garrisons he'd been in over the last moons. About what people wore, what they ate, how they celebrated this or that holiday. He colored in her world, adding details she craved about the world outside the walls.

"One day I want to travel down to Shelter City. Stay for a while. Stand on the shores of the Great Sea."

"It smells so clean. Like nothing else. The sand, so soft, like a cloud, aye? And the water chases away and rushes back. Over and over. Nipping at your toes. Cool and fresh. You'd like it."

People did travel for holiday. They could book space on official transport, but the price was dear and there was a wait list. A very long one. Extremely difficult too, for unaccompanied women unless they were visiting to be courted. She frowned at the idea.

She dried the last of the dishes and hung the towel on the peg.

"Would you like some music then?"

"I would. I brought you some books as well."

She smiled. When he visited he not only brought her little indulgences, but important things like books and periodicals. She loved to read and he did as well. He brought her all manner of things, from light and breezy stories of fancy and love to heavier, darker tales. Reference manuals she kept in her kitchen shelves. She traded the books around the garrison and they ended up in the library when she was done. She wasn't the only one who loved to read.

"Thank you."

Her music player was charged and soft music played through the room after she hit the switch. He'd built a fire earlier so the living room was cozy and warm. He handed her a large bundle and she settled on her settee to look through the titles as he settled in the large chair and pulled the newspaper out.

It was so lovely. Normal and yet a rare treat, as he'd be gone in just days and she'd be alone here once more. His smell filled the space and she breathed it deep, wanting to be bold enough to tell him how much she wanted him to touch her. Damning the world she'd been raised in, the world that had kept her from knowledge, had raised her to always use soft words, to keep her gaze averted and to wait for the man to do the talking and action taking.

It was a silly world and it had raised silly women all chafing at the rules that were supposed to protect them. From what no one ever seemed to want to tell her.

She only knew she was fortunate not to be under a man's thumb any longer. Her independence came at a cost. A price she'd pay a thousand times over to be in her own place, on her own terms. One she also realized wouldn't last forever, but she planned to enjoy it as long as she could.

"Loyal?"

He looked up, awaiting her question. He wasn't one of the silly men who'd fluttered around with flattery and charming smiles to talk her into sneaking a kiss, or far more. No, he didn't waste words except when he told her the stories about the outside world.

"Are women like this all through the Highway?"

He folded the paper once and then another time, sitting it in his lap. "How do you mean?"

"Overprotected, aye? Taught to only speak the sweetest of words?"

He struggled with a smile and she narrowed her eyes his way.

"There are garrisons where the women are not allowed to come out when we arrive. Where women cannot be unescorted by a male. Others where the women are equals, who have the same rights as the men. Silver Cliffs is a garrison on that side of the continuum, though not as open-minded as Shelter City."

"Hm." She nodded. "I wish to visit those places."

"Have some hard words you need to use, then?"

"Are you making fun?"

He laughed, the sound rusty, but lovely and welcome. "I would never dream of such a thing."

He picked his paper back up. "Should you like to use the bad words or get up to things men do, feel free. I can even offer you assistance should you need it."

Boldness burst through her. "Yes? Say if I wanted you to put your lips on mine then? Would you do that?"

His gaze snagged on hers. "I don't think that's a good idea."

"Is that so? And why is that?"

"Because you are fine and beautiful. You are feminine and graceful and I am not."

"If I had want of another woman I could find one and ask her for a kiss, Lawman."

He blushed for a moment, swallowing hard. "You know what I mean."

"No, I really don't. Do you not have a wanting of me? A woman back home?"

He licked his lips. "My wanting of you is not the issue. I'm not for you."

He went back to his paper and left her frowning.

Confused and frustrated.

But also, the fire in her belly lit. She saw it in his gaze. He wanted her and now curiosity and stubbornness worked together.

She wanted Loyal Alsbaugh.

CHAPTER THREE

SHE DECIDED to go ahead and take a bath once he'd retired to his room. It would be an early start for her come morning. She'd get up, wash her face, braid her hair and, after a quick breakfast, would spend the rest of her day rushed off her feet in the mercantile.

The water was nice and hot as she disrobed before pinning her hair up. A few drops of oil in the water filled the room with scented steam, relaxing her.

Well. Most of her.

Just being around him sent butterflies into her belly and a bone-deep knowledge that if she should ever be so lucky to have him in her bed she'd never be the same. Loyal was the kind of man who would know what to do.

She sighed as she stepped in, groaning a little at how good the water had felt. The wine and company had loosened her muscles and the water did the rest.

Starting at her toes, she slid her hands and the cloth over her skin until she had to catch her breath at her mid thigh.

Her legs parted as she thought of his hands. The way he'd felt when he'd helped her up on the platform out back once before. Strong. And yet he touched her like she was precious. Not fragile, despite his earlier tease; he seemed to respect that she was capable and intelligent. But special.

Once, when she'd first been married to James, he'd rutted and passed out and she'd escaped the house, heading out for a long walk. And she'd seen Bethany Schaffer with Abel Temple. He'd pressed her up against the side of his house. Into a shadowed corner. If she hadn't been where she was, coming down the street quietly, she doubted anyone else could have seen.

But *she* had. She'd ducked behind a tree and watched with envy, knowing she'd never have that, not with James and his sour whiskey breath and his mean, careless fingers.

But the fingers she brushed against her pussy weren't his. Not anymore. Her fingers knew what she liked, what she wanted as they slid her labia apart, remembering how Bethany and Abel had looked together that night.

And the memory changed, shifted into fantasy as Bethany's eyes became Verity's, those hands sweeping up and over Bethany's breasts became Loyal's.

She soaped over her belly, one hand remaining at her pussy. She brushed the pad of her middle finger over her clit, breathing in deep as the wave of pleasure rippled outward.

The other hand tested the weight of her breast, a slippery thumb flicked back and forth over her nipple. Her eyes drifted closed.

His mouth would find her nipple, suck and draw until she rolled her hips, seeking more. He'd slide his hand down into her drawers, petting and then finding her hot and wet.

A teasing touch of his fingertip against her clit, all while his mouth was still on her nipple.

She'd whimper softly, urging him for more. Because she'd need more. And he'd give it to her with a snarl as he spread her legs apart with a knee. The teasing touch on her clit would turn into a gentle pinch of thumb and forefinger.

His cock would brush against her, pressing in just right until she arched her back on a gasp as he thrust all the way, all while he concentrated on her clit.

He'd whisper how much he wanted her, how sexy she was, how good she felt. His words a hot brush of breath against her nipple as he bit gently.

He'd fuck her like she'd dreamed all these years. She'd be the woman whose man took her as she threw her legs around his waist, her head falling back as she bit her lip, coming hard as he continued to thrust until he found his own end moments later.

LOYAL HAD BEEN STANDING at the window, staring out over the town, smoking and trying very hard not to think about Verity's suggestion that he kiss her.

He'd wanted to. Had even thought of ways to do it to teach her a lesson. But that would have been dishonest. And unfair to use that when she'd been chafing at the ways she'd felt restricted as a woman.

Especially when he wanted to kiss her so badly the hand holding the cigar shook a little.

She rustled in the bathroom next door and he tried not to imagine her in there, disrobing. All that pale, pretty skin exposed.

The scent of her soap, or whatever it was she was using, seeped under the door along with the steam.

He undressed, usually sleeping naked if he were home or in a hotel. But because he was there in her guest room, he kept his drawers on, along with his undershirt.

He was tired. Been on the road long enough that his muscles had ached for hours once he'd arrived. That had passed, but the exhaustion remained, blunted by the excellent dinner and company. He carefully stubbed the end of his cigar, saving the rest for the next day. He needed to sleep.

And that's when he heard the groan.

He scrubbed a hand over his face at the sound.

There was a splash here and there, enough he knew she was settling in the tub. The night was quiet enough that once he'd slid into bed, he could hear the sound of the water as she soaped herself up.

He lay there. Imagining her, slick and wet.

No. Fuck. No.

He tried to think on other things and then he heard it, another moan, only this was not a feel good sitting in the bath groan. No, he'd heard the sound come from a woman's lips as she'd been underneath him often enough to know. It was a moan of pleasure.

Which meant she was... The breath shot from his lungs. She had her hands on her pussy, on nipples he'd imagined way more than once or twice. She was just on the other side of the wall, making herself climax.

He should have put a pillow over his head and gone to sleep.

Instead, his hand found its way down to his cock, freeing it. Still hard from earlier, revived by the sound of her naked and touching herself just on the other side of a door.

She'd be a pale beauty, her breasts buoyed in the water, her nipples —they'd be cinnamon pink, he wagered—would peek just above the water line.

Knees up, perhaps?

He fisted himself, imagining slamming the door open.

"Seems to me, Verity, you need a cock deep inside you. No hand is going to make you feel the way I can."

She'd blush, caught with one hand delving between her thighs, the other frozen on her nipple.

He squeezed his cock harder, finding a rhythm.

He'd stalk over and pull her to stand as he sat on the side of her tub. He'd pull her down into his lap, right onto his cock. It'd be tight, that sweet cunt of hers. Most likely ripple around him as he seated himself fully.

Oh the sound she'd make. He cupped his balls with his free hand, speeding the grip on his cock as he imagined pumping into her body. The way her lips would part so he could kiss her, the taste of her as his tongue lapped at her.

"Later I'm going to lick your pussy just like this."

He had to bite his lip to keep back a groan at the thought of his face between her legs. He'd lay odds that old bastard she'd been tied to never ate her out. Never tasted her sweetness that way.

He heard her gasp next door. Heard a soft moan as the water splashed. Knew she was coming. Wondering if she thought of him as she did. Knowing, even as he told himself it was bad, that she did.

He arched, the hot, wet evidence of his climax hitting his hand as he worked to stay quiet, as he listened to her, thought about the way it would feel to come as he thrust so deep inside her body.

HOW OLD WERE you when you were married?" He asked her this as they walked side by side up the hill back from the picnic the garrison had just held for the lawmen and transit drivers.

She looked at him askance briefly. "I was fourteen."

He frowned.

"My parents felt I was willful. Said I'd settle once I got married and had children. Thank the heavens James wasn't able to put a baby in my belly," she mumbled.

He raised a brow at her impertinence, liking it.

"Oh I know I'm supposed to want all that. And maybe I would have with another man. All getting married at fourteen did was make me hate my parents and end up dodging fists and tripping over sick and empty bottles for the next eight annum until he ended up dead at the end of a knife, bleeding out in an alley. No one missed him for three days."

"There were no good times then?" He shook his head. "Forgive my intrusiveness."

She waved it away. "Despite what I was raised to think and feel, I am not ashamed of what he was, or what he did to me. It was his sin, not mine. The blessing is that I have a way to remain independent now. My parents are dead. I did my duty and married. No one can force me into it again. No one can take my property. I'm a widow so that means they have to leave me alone for the time being. So I suppose that would qualify as a good time."

He'd never met anyone like her. Fiery and yet soft and sweet all at once. All that contradiction only made him yearn for her all the harder.

"So you're off tomorrow morning then?"

"Yes. Two more stops to make and then we start over at Shelter City."

"When will you be back?"

"Transports will be more frequent now that the weather is better. A moon or two most likely unless we pick up anything for Silver Cliffs in Charity Bay or Northern Tip."

"I wish I could come along."

He briefly let himself imagine her next to him as he drove. She'd most likely be a good companion on the long stretches of roadway. And then he remembered the fear, the heart-pounding danger the brigands posed him and his team several times every annum. The reason they all had to live behind walls.

"It's dangerous out there. I'd never want that life for you. Here you're safe. You can walk out in the sunshine. Have citrus punch and eat cakes. No one is trying to harm you."

"It's the same. Year after year. There's a whole world out there and I'm not living in it. You're out there and I'm not. I like having you around."

She blushed and he may have done so as well. As much as a man like him could.

"We'll be back before you know it. I'll be smoking in your spare room and eating all your eggs."

She shrugged. "Sure."

"It's your last night here. I won't be offended if you wish to join your friends down at the bar."

He snorted. "If I wished to have a drink with them, I could most days." He was of the opinion that it was best not to get drunk with the townsfolk of the garrisons they were responsible for protecting. They were supposed to be seen a certain way. Part of that was to hold themselves apart. It was hard to do that if you sat ass to ass on bar stools. Townies didn't need to see a lawman drink to excess. Though to be fair to his team, he doubted that would happen. They knew their jobs.

Moreover, he'd far rather have Verity all to himself his last evening in Silver Cliffs. He'd had to watch all day long as she helped with the preparation for the large cookout they'd had. Watched as men took her in with greedy eyes. And why not? There was something so very vibrant about her that others couldn't begin to match.

One of these days he'd come back through those big garrison gates and she'd be courted, or maybe even married to someone. And while it was an honor to lodge a lawman, he wasn't sure how he'd feel about sitting at her dinner table with another man at the head. A man who touched her in all the places Loyal dreamed of.

"All right then. You did promise to teach me a new card game. The last time you were here, remember? I have ale and some of the sweets left over from the luncheon today."

"Aye, that sounds like a very fine evening. I'm sure the men in town would thank me for teaching you how to be a card sharp."

She laughed, delighted. "That would be lovely indeed. I could build up a savings on the side to travel if I could do that."

"Travel?"

"I'm saving to visit Shelter City. I'm a ways off from a buy in for the waitlist. But I figure if I have another two good annum I can do it." She pulled a deck of cards from a drawer in her buffet cabinet and held them aloft.

"I'll get the ale." He headed into her kitchen. A woman like her in the capital would attract a lot of attention. A man would have to be blind to miss her.

"I'll be back in a moment. I'm going to change."

She stood in front of her closet, peering inside, frustrated. She *knew* he was interested in her in a romantic way. He watched her at times, the way men did women they fancied. He paused when she talked about travel or when she'd related the story about John William trying to argue her into letting him court her the season before.

But he kept his distance no matter.

It made her want to stomp her foot and toss a fit, is what it did. Though she was far too old for such silliness. And too smart. She knew that too.

Verity had to figure out how to shake him up, how to get him to abandon his silly insistence on not kissing her. Or bedding her. Or anything fun like that.

She pulled on a soft, long-sleeved blouse and some trousers. She unpinned and unplaited her hair, deciding to leave it loose around her shoulders before heading back out to her living room where he'd poured them both a goblet of ale and built a fire.

"Thank you for taking care of the fire. Clear skies mean cold nights this time of the season. A fair exchange I suppose, especially when the woodstove heats the house so nicely."

He stared at her long and hard without speaking and self-consciousness swept through her. "Is all well?"

He cleared his throat. "Yes, yes, I apologize for staring. Your hair . . . you . . . I don't know that I've seen it loose like that before."

She blushed, reaching up to touch it. "Does it look funny?"

He shook his head. "No. It's beautiful. Like sunset. Not a color you see often up and down the highway."

Warmth spread through her at the compliment. "Thank you. I have so much of it and it's so curly I keep it up or pinned back usually. My mother's hair was this color. My sister's is dark like my father's was. I guess . . . I guess you knew that as you've seen her around."

He pulled her chair out and she sat.

"I quite prefer yours." He studiously avoided her gaze as he spoke, pulling the cards from the leather case.

She sipped her ale, trying not to be nervous. Not nervous, actually, sort of . . . giddy. Yes, giddy. He'd taken notice of her in that way of his. But it was hard for him to shake off this time. She smiled at him when he looked up.

"That smile should make me nervous."

"Ah, but does it, mighty lawman? Do I make you nervous?"

He laughed then, hearty, a sound she rarely heard from him. "Any smart man would be advised to remain nervous around a beautiful woman who smiles like she's got a secret. It's what they call evolutionary learning, aye? Now, on to cards. We can't neglect your card sharp training."

They played cards for several hours as she coaxed stories from him about his travels. He rarely liked to speak about himself but she did something to him. Loosened him up before he even realized it. It was nice to let his guard down around her. To feel safe within the walls of her cozy home and simply be Loyal.

She cleaned up, preparing everything for the next morning as she usually did, and for a moment he allowed himself to imagine this with her. This with her as his woman. Frivolous, and a waste of time, he tried to argue with himself, but he did it anyway.

She turned back to him once she'd finished. "I'm to bed. Since you're all leaving tomorrow there'll be a flurry of things to take care of. You know how people are. Always waiting too long to do the necessaries."

He nodded. It was the same in every garrison. The morning they left the townspeople would line up to get those last-minute letters and packages on the transport. The bits and bobs they wanted to barter with others up and down the highway.

"Human nature."

She stepped closer but he'd been leaning against the doorway to his room so he had no place to step away. Her scent wrapped around him, a fist of the glory of her womanhood, and he could do nothing but let it.

"I'll miss you."

He had to clear his throat to get the words out as she stood close enough that her hair brushed the back of his hand where his arms were crossed over his chest. Flowers and sunshine and a tiny bit of wood smoke. The spice of his cigar was what got him the most. His scent had marked her in a sense and though he didn't want to, he found himself moved by it. His cock hardened.

"I'll be back afore you know it. You stay safe. Brigand reports not too far down the Highway. Stay behind the walls."

"I can't always do that."

"You need to."

She went to her tiptoes. "And what'll you give me if I do?" Her breasts brushed against his forearms and he groaned, grabbing her upper arms before he knew it, hauling her that tiny bit closer and his mouth came down on hers.

She moaned, opening up to his tongue as it swept into her mouth. She was sweet and hot, eager as he took and took. There was no artifice about her. She wasn't an expert at kissing, but what she lacked in experience she more than made up for in enthusiasm.

Even as his brain screamed at him to stop, his heart, his bones, his cock, everything he felt with urged him to take. To seduce and tease.

Her taste slid through his veins, gripping, digging in and rooting itself deep.

She made a startled sound—not distress—excitement, desire, when he nipped her bottom lip. He'd been trying to pull away, but the sound brought him back for more. Gods, more and more.

He kissed his way over her jaw, feasted on the spot just below her ear until she made another sound, a gasp of his name.

With every last bit of strength he possessed, he set her back from him, licking his lips as she looked up at him, dazed, her mouth kiss-swollen, skin flushed. So beautiful and carnal.

"I'm sorry." His chest seemed to burn as he fought his instinct to take her to the bed, to strip her of all her clothes and feast on her skin.

"Why?"

"This can't happen."

She frowned. "Ridiculous. It just *did* happen. I liked it. You liked it. Why shouldn't it happen more?"

"I already told you, I am not for you. Go to bed, Verity. Go to bed and thank your heavens above that I have the strength to make the right decision here." He pushed her back slightly to get around her and inside his room where he could close the door before he made any more mistakes.

CHAPTER FOUR

WHEN SHE'D WOKEN UP, he'd already packed his things and gone. A look out the windows showed the transport and escort vehicles lined up.

She didn't speed her pace. It was early still. She made herself breakfast and drank some tea before heading down to the mercantile and opening up. She handled all the last-minute packages and other mail and with Tobin, organized people into orderly lines to hand over their things to the transport drivers.

She caught sight of Loyal down the way at the garrison offices with the other members of his team. He looked up the hill and saw her, nodding his head. She waved, but kept at her work. The night before had simply been step one. He'd awakened something in her she hadn't even really known she possessed.

A sort of carnal awakening, a sense of her own power as a woman. She'd made him short of breath. She'd brought him so much need his fingers had dug into her upper arms hard enough to leave two fingerprint bruises. Not that she'd mention it. She got the feeling he would feel guilty and she didn't want that.

It had filled her with a sort of satisfaction to see them. To see the effect of the loss of his control. His need had washed over her skin like a narcotic of sorts.

Loyal Alsbaugh wanted her. With so much ferocity it had set her aflame just being in contact with his body. She wanted more. Knew when it happened—and it would— it would change her. And hopefully him as well.

She could wait. For the time being in any case.

The townspeople used to the process of the leaving of the transport had been orderly and ready as their turn had come. Verity handed over the mail sacks and signed them in for delivery.

They'd all congregate shortly down at the bottom of the hill at the gates. But she moved to the lead vehicle where Loyal had just locked his rifle into the slot on the dash.

"You stay safe. And return soon. You didn't finish your card lessons."

He shook his head, a half smile on his mouth. A mouth that had been on her own, on her neck. A shiver went though her at the memory.

"Stay in the garrison like I said, aye? Please?"

She knew what that please must have cost him, so she nodded. "As much as I can, I will. Come back soon."

"Safe travels." He got in the vehicle.

"And to you." She stepped back to the walk and watched him close the door and click the side shield into place over the window.

"I don't know how they do it. How they face the dangers of that Highway each and every time the way they do." Tobin said it with some greed as he watched the procession head down the hill.

Perhaps she wasn't the only one in the family with a curiosity about the world outside.

"They do it because it needs doing." She waved at the transport and then the vehicles at the rear of the procession.

There were shouts and horns sounding at the gate as the sentries called out the all clear and the wheels began to turn as the gate slid to the side. Each vehicle drove through until they were all out. She knew they'd cross the bridge singly and then head down the fortified road to the Highway and drive north.

Her old life clicked back into place as the gate did.

"Come along then, Tobin. We've got some inventory to do."

SHE'D SPENT her time immersed in all the daily work she needed to do to get ready for the coming seasons. Out behind the mercantile she spent her late afternoons after she'd closed down tilling the soil and getting her planting rows in order.

She planted her seeds for the melons and root-based vegetables. Those she kept in the cellar below the store. The cool earth would keep them through the snow times. She'd be able to use them in soups and stews, baked in casseroles all through the coldest months. She trimmed back all her berry bushes near the low walls that separated her land from her neighbor's. Those would burst into life in a few moons and keep her in pies and preserves for the rest of the annum and also give her plenty to trade.

She opened all the parcels that had come with the delivery. Read the letters from her far-flung friends at garrisons up and down the Highway. She always saved them until he'd gone. For those first, hardest weeks when she felt his absence the deepest. There were little bottles of perfumed water, pots of healing salves for burns and rashes, muslin bags of dried herbs. Jars of preserves, of sauces, of flavored spreads to put on game and fish. Most she'd keep for herself, as they were little trades in return for her jars and bags of things she'd created. Others she'd use as payment for goods and services in the garrison throughout the annum. When her machinery needed fixing, or when she needed extra labor in the mercantile.

Over the weeks she'd received several blips from the central governance. Reports of increased brigand attacks on Highway traffic. And two incursions on garrisons.

Jackson Haldeman, the head of the garrison defense, showed up at the mercantile just as she was closing up. "Good day, Verity." He tipped his head and she smiled.

"Hello, Jackson. Do you have need of something from inside? I know the proprietor so I can open up for you."

He laughed, his smile spreading over his features, making him very handsome indeed.

"Appreciate that. But no. Not today. I came to let you know that, if you'd like, we're going to be doing some instruction. With the rifles. I know you have some first aid education and if you'd be of a mind to teach others, I'd see it as a kindness. With the increase in brigand attacks, I want to stay at the ready."

"Of course. To both. I know how to shoot. But I could use more instruction. I just put by some healing herbs and salves. I can make extras for the garrison barracks as well. They keep if you leave them in a cool, dry place. A root cellar or the like."

He nodded. "Thank you. On the morrow then, an hour before the sun sets we'll be starting with target practice."

"I'll be there. I can do some lessons on dressing wounds and the like on the off days. With harvest season ahead, it's a good knowledge. Always end up with injuries that time of year in any case."

He nodded. Pausing. His gaze sliding over her face with pleasure.

If it weren't for Loyal, would she wish he'd invite her for a walk? Should she go if he invited her? He would be a good catch, as her sister would say. Jackson with his broad shoulders and his easy smile. A provider. She'd never heard tales of him hitting the bottle or anyone else.

"I'll see you tomorrow then." He stepped down. "And perhaps . . . perhaps I will be seeing you at the fest this coming week's end?"

The fish were running. Every year the big, fat silver fish would come in high numbers to the river to lay their eggs and have lots of tiny baby silver fish. The town would net them and set them to smoke, to dry them, to jar them in oils and herbs and preserve them for the annum ahead. It was a unified effort. There was music in the evenings and a big dance out under the stars.

"Aye." She smiled, not really knowing exactly what she was agreeing to other than the target practice.

CHAPTER FIVE

SHE'D BEEN TOTING her rifle over to the field behind the garrison offices when she heard the horn sounding at the main gates.

She noted that the field was empty, so they must have all gone down already. Wisely, she kept the rifle. The horn wasn't the friendly note of non-hostile traffic, though not the alarm either.

She caught sight of Tobin. "Go back home."

"Why? I want to see who it is."

"Because there've been blip bulletins about the brigands attacking up and down the Highway lately. Because I said so and I'm your aunt, that's why."

He frowned.

"If it's bad, you'll need to be in a place you can hunker down and protect your family. Now get on home."

He nodded, grumbling, but he turned and headed back toward home. That was one less worry.

Men weren't running down the hill with rifles so that was a plus, but she headed up to her parlor to look out and saw the tail end of the procession. Lawmen.

Her heart skipped a beat and she put her rifle back in the closet and headed to her porch.

It had only been a moon since they were in Silver Cliffs last. Happiness replaced her worry at the rare treat to be able to see him again so soon.

The gates rumbled open as she watched.

Not the usual large official transport though. A smaller one. They used to be that size back when she was younger and the deliveries came about once a moon. The time between deliveries had lengthened as she'd gotten older.

Clearly something had changed. She wondered if it was a good thing or not.

Tobin came running up just a few moments later. "Guess I better get the mercantile open."

"Doesn't look like we'll be taking in a large order. But yes, let's get the back doors open and see what we're dealing with."

LOYAL PULLED up to the garrison offices and got out. One of the vehicles remained at the gates until they'd closed and would be along in a bit.

Haldeman came out with a wave. "Weren't expecting you back so soon. Everything all right?"

"Brigand attacks increasing. I suppose you been hearing?"

Haldeman nodded. "We've been doing target practice frequently to keep everyone sharp. Extra patrols. Verity has been doing triage and first aid for those wanting the lessons. Course, a pretty woman teaching you how to sew up a wound makes for some full classes."

Loyal wanted to snarl at the idea, but held it back. Nodding. Because he understood it. The world was dark sometimes. Hard living in these garrisons. Lots of work. You took your pleasures when you could get them. And most certainly looking at Verity Coleman would count as a pleasure.

"More lawmen out. They've cut our territory down, added two more escorts to each sector of the Highway. Figure it's better to let them see our increased presence and to keep folks happy with more mail and the like." And shorter trips for the escort edged the danger back a smidge, even as it filled the Highway with more guns and men and women who'd use them to protect those they were charged to protect.

"About a dozen annum back, aye? We had a lot of attacks then too. That's when we added the fortifications to the road leading up from the Highway. Is it that bad now?"

"Don't rightly know just yet. But if you can afford to add to your patrols, you should. Keep people up in those towers full time. They're leaving the Highway to come to the garrisons more and more often. Maybe they have a baby boom." He shrugged. They didn't know a whole lot about the brigands. They were nomads in nature, moving in large encampments.

He'd been a tracker first, before he'd hit the Highway with his escort team. Throughout history, especially after the big tech war, the central governance had tried to reach out to the brigands, to offer them land to set up, help with crops and the like. Urging them to leave peaceably. But what the governance had been confronted with was that the brigands weren't the same. They didn't want to settle. They *liked* their raids. Seemed to embrace the bloodlust of preying on the weak, of the raping and killing.

They were human still, yes, but not fully. There was something different. Less . . . civilized he supposed. And they had no hesitation in the burning and the pillaging of anything they could.

"I'm on it then. I'll be able to find you at the mercantile later?"

Loyal knew he should stay there at the barracks. After that kiss—and gods knew he'd thought about it constantly since he'd left—he should keep his distance. But he wouldn't. Couldn't.

He turned, catching sight of that sunset red as she took delivery of the mail. "Yes. I'm available to help with your patrols as well. We'll be here three days."

"I'll be up later then." Haldeman smiled as he looked up the hill. "Think I'll be getting the mail for my mother. Always nice to have an excuse to chat a spell with the widow Coleman."

Loyal wanted to punch the other man for even thinking about her. Instead, he nodded again and tried to keep his expression neutral. "All right."

He left his vehicle near the garrison and met up with the rest of his people.

"I've offered our services to Haldeman with the patrols. Trinity, I want you to be sure they're at least taking the opportunity to track on occasion. Bren, you work with them on their hand to hand. Marcus, take a look at their sentry points outside the walls. Haldeman says he's working on target practice so I imagine Indigo can help with that. Not tonight. Everyone get some rest tonight. Let's be sure we leave Silver Cliffs safer than we found it."

He headed up the hill, knowing she'd be there, needing it more than he should have.

The line for mail was the usual and he waited his turn. She caught sight of him and smiled. A smile just for him. "Head on up. I didn't know you'd be arriving, so there's no basket of baked goods. There's fresh bread on cooling racks in the pantry, though. I'll be up later."

He nodded and headed around back.

SHE MANAGED to get finished and to close up within the hour. Since the delivery had come so late, most folks would wait until the following day to pick up their orders, which worked for her as she was hungry and tired.

And she wanted to see him.

The scent of his cigar hit her as she climbed to her front door. He sat at her kitchen table with a mug of tea at his left hand, a sheaf of papers before him on the table. She noted the red stamp at the top. Sealed blips, she noted. She delivered those—unread— to the garrison when they came. And there'd been a lot of them as of late.

"Good evening, lawman."

"Good evening, Ms. Coleman."

She squeezed his shoulder as she moved past. "Are you hungry then?"

"I am."

"I'll make us some supper and you can tell me what's happening with this new schedule."

She pushed her sleeves up and washed her hands before she began to pull together a meal.

"You're too bright for your own good."

She laughed. "If only you were the first person to tell me such nonsense. How is one too smart for their own good? In any case, I can read the blips. I know there are more attacks. Your change in schedule is most likely due to that. It's not mysterious."

"Aye. They've put more lawmen out on the Highway. It's good for citizens to see us, to know they're protected. But the shift only just happened a week ago so there's been some scrambling. We made a big jump and drove straight through without stopping. Stayed in Salt Flats two nights though, so it's better than we were before that."

"And how long are you here this time?"

"We're staying in all mid-sized garrisons three days now. Small ones we'll do overnights. The largest we stay for two days. My team will accompany patrols, do sentry duty."

"Good training for the garrison soldiers here. To see how you all do your job in that setting. Most of them are farmers. Aside from the full-time garrison sentries." She paused as she deposited a bowl of sliced fruit on the table. "It's bad then? Risky?"

"There's been a great deal of activity along this sector. We don't think you're at risk for an assault, but it won't hurt for their scouts to see us on the ramparts of the garrison walls."

"All right then."

"Been busy since I last left?"

"Gearing up for—" There was a knock on the back door. "Can you get that then? I need to turn the fish when it's ready."

He stood, moving carefully to the door.

Jackson Haldeman stood there with a smile. "Well met, Loyal."

Loyal stood aside to let Jackson in, hiding a frown as he headed straight to the kitchen.

Verity smiled when she saw who it was. "Good evening, Jackson. I was just making some supper. Would you like to stay?"

Jackson's expression lit in an entirely different way when gave his attentions to Verity. His smile softened as he took her in from head to toe. "I would very much, thank you."

That's when Loyal realized Jackson Haldeman had his eye on Verity as more than a passing fancy.

"I'll get another place set." Loyal moved past Haldeman to grab another plate and some utensils. He put them on the side away from Verity.

Jackson held up a sack. "I brought some sweets. My mother wanted to thank you for the poultice you made for her leg."

Verity took the bag and peeked inside. "Spiced fried dough? Your mother knows my weakness. We'll have them after dinner. Sit. Both of you."

She filled their plates with food and sat, chattering about her day and whatever else was going on for some time until she finally sat back. "All right then. I'm sure you're here for an official reason, Jackson. Go on."

"You might as well speak plainly in front of her or she'll pester you until you do."

Verity's surprised laughter came right as Loyal realized he'd spoken his thoughts aloud. He gave her a stern look but she waved it away and kept eating.

He and Jackson spoke then about their plans. About the news that the brigands had attacked Banyon Pass two days prior. The garrison had managed to repel the attack, but not without losing a third of its livestock and nearly twenty citizens.

Banyon Pass was roughly the same size as Silver Cliffs, though it wasn't quite as protected by the surrounding landscape as silver cliffs was.

"Why are they suddenly so much more active?" she asked.

"We don't know. It's always like this. It ebbs and flows, aye? We can go an annum or three with minimal activity and then suddenly they're everywhere, attacking. We don't know much about the other side of the mountains." Just that it was fairly inhospitable and crawling with brigands.

"I've got a meeting set for just after breakfast. Come down to the garrison offices and you can address my people. We'll double our patrols. I've already doubled the sentries on the walls."

"Smart."

Jackson stood. "I need to get back home. Thank you for dinner, Verity."

She smiled at him. "Thank you for the sweets. And your mother. If she needs more of the poultice let me know. I'm teaching a few in town how to make them and it's good practice."

He disappeared with one last nod at Loyal and a promise to see him the following morning.

"Looks like Haldeman has an eye on you."

She looked Loyal's way, one of her brows hiking. "Yes, I believe he does. Question is, Loyal, what are you going to do about that?"

"What do you mean?"

"I mean, you look like you just sucked on a lemon. Clearly you don't like it that Jackson is sweet on me. And I'm asking what you plan to do about it."

She moved out of the kitchen, pulling her curtains closed here and there as she moved through the house. He wandered behind her, breathing her in.

"I . . . Nothing, I suppose."

She spun, stomped over and poked him in the chest. "Nothing?"

"Are you sweet on him?"

"I'm on fire for you." Her voice was low. Urgent. Full of emotion and it set his world on its end. "There's no sweet on him, no room for that. Not when every time I think of you I can remember what it felt like to have your mouth on mine."

He licked his lips. Knowing he should step back. *Knowing it.* But he didn't.

"You shouldn't be. He's a better choice. Safer. He's here. I'm not."

She made a sound, frustrated. "Since when does that sort of thing ever play into it? I'm not my sister. I can't place my affections, my desire, based on a set of calculations about which man would come with more cows and pigs, who could chop more wood to keep my home warm through the snow. My desire doesn't care about that. It cares about the way your voice changes, deepens when I stand this close. How your scent rises to my nose as your skin heats. Spicy like your cigars. How when I see your vehicle my entire system seems to come alive and I realize all the time when you are not here is gray. You make me feel alive, Loyal. So stand there, why don't you, and tell me what you plan to do about Jackson Haldeman wanting to court me. Hm?"

He should have told her to back off. Hells, he should have backed off himself, retreated to his room and closed the door.

Instead, he slid his hands around her neck and yanked her close, his mouth falling on hers like he needed it more than his very breath. Which he was fairly certain was true.

She sighed, her body molding to his, her posture softening, submitting to his control and that only made his need worse. The roar of it harder to overcome and so he ignored all the voices telling him to stop and continued to plunder the sweetness of her mouth.

He sucked her tongue and she gasped and then moaned, arching. Irresistible. The need to show her what a real man could do in bed, how he could love her until she was boneless, raced through him. He wanted to show her that. He wanted to make her come so hard she sobbed, and the idea that anyone else wanted to do that, wanted to lay with her at night drove him on, drove him to burn into her memory just how much he desired her.

Wanted her to never forget him.

And it didn't matter that he shouldn't. It didn't matter that he'd told himself for years not to let himself get carried away with what he felt for Verity Coleman.

All that mattered was the need that beat at him, the way her breath hitched, the way her fingers had tangled in his hair, holding him close as he continued to kiss her.

Knowing a kiss, even hours' worth of kisses would not be enough.

Her grip tightened in his hair, bringing a grunt to his lips as he pulled her snug to his body, rolling his hips to let her know what was happening. Maybe on some level trying to scare her into breaking away. If she pushed him back or broke this off he could find the strength to end it.

He sure didn't have it on his own.

Instead she made a soft sound and pressed closer still, brushing her body against his cock, setting off licks of flame through his belly, low, hot, electric.

She let go of his hair and pulled back a tiny bit, but only to get her hands at the buttons on his uniform shirt. Unfastening quickly until she slid it open all the way, her palms caressing all the skin she'd bared.

It was his turn to groan, to hitch a breath as she pressed the heels of her hands against his nipples. She paused, breaking the kiss. "Yes? You like that?"

Surprising him, she pushed him back against the doorjamb and leaned, licking over his nipple. Gently at first.

"Harder."

Her eyes cut to him and she pressed her tongue, flicking it against his right nipple. Scoring her teeth over it until he gasped.

She kissed over his chest to his left nipple, kissing, licking that one until he hauled her back up, taking her mouth once more.

Then he pulled her blouse from the waist of her trousers and parted it, untying the ribbons holding it closed until she was left only in a chemise, the shadow of her nipples visible through the translucent material.

"So beautiful."

She swallowed hard, looking up at him as he looked down at her breasts. He cupped them briefly before he pulled the tiny, pearly buttons from the holes, one after the next until he stared at her, at the luscious swell of breasts he'd dreamed of since the first time he laid eyes on the widow Coleman.

"Better than dreams."

The hesitance washed from her face, replaced by a boldness that made him even harder.

"Touch me, Loyal."

He did. Brushing his thumbs over the hardened nipples until she arched. He kissed down her neck as he shifted, backing her into his room. To the bed he laid in when he was there, fantasizing this exact thing. Only now it was real.

She reached out as she hit the mattress, pulling him down with her.

"Don't go anywhere."

He pulled his shirt off, toeing his shoes away as he did. "I'm not. I have far too many things to do."

She unbuttoned the side of her trousers and shimmied out of them as he did the same with his pants.

The moon was high overhead, casting silvery light over her skin, now totally bare.

"You're so pretty, Verity." He swallowed hard, sliding his hands over the curve at her hips.

She grabbed his cock, squeezing gently. "You too."

"I'm . . . pretty?" He'd meant it to be a joke, but she'd slid her thumb through the slick at the crown and it sent a shock of pleasure through him, sending his words scattering from his head like birds going into flight.

"In your way, yes. Manly. Hard and strong."

He moved back to the bed, laying next to her. "I shouldn't be doing this."

"You plan to stop?"

He shook his head. "Not unless you want me to."

"I want your hands on me. Show me, Loyal. Teach me how to make you feel good. I'm not . . . not like the ladies you likely bed when you land in their garrisons."

"You aren't. Which is why you're impossible to resist."

She smiled and he pulled her hair loose so it fell against her pale skin like rivers of flame.

"And you're doing just fine at making me feel good."

She laughed.

"Now I want to make *you* feel good."

He bent to her again, kissing her mouth, nipping and licking until she was breathless. He left her lips and kissed over her face and down to her chin. Delicate and yet, as he'd realized after knowing her as long as he had, strong.

He licked over the hollow behind her jaw and she shuddered a sigh.

"Like that?" he murmured against that sweet, sensitive space.

"Y-Yes."

He continued, kissing down her neck, his hands sliding over her chest, over her collarbone, down to her breasts—those glorious breasts. He tugged and rolled her nipples until she made a sound unlike any he'd ever heard her make. A sound he knew without a doubt he'd never forget. Full of need and pleasure.

He licked over one nipple as he tugged on the other. He sucked. Gently and then harder. When he bit she gasped and then her entire body seemed to heat.

She liked it hard.

He was in trouble.

Because he liked it hard too.

He tried again, a little rougher, pulling her nipple with his teeth as he moved back and she moaned, her hips jutting forward as she did.

He did this to the other nipple as she held on at his shoulder, her short nails digging in until he groaned.

He kissed over her ribs, across her belly and breathed over her mound.

She froze, the weight of the moment on them both.

He slid her thighs wide as he moved to the floor, settling on his knees between them, pulling her butt to the edge of the bed.

She gasped. "Oh. I"

He kissed the back of her knee. Her skin smelled like nothing else he'd ever experienced. Hot and spicy and sweet. Up her thigh until he blew against her cunt.

He heard her swallow there in the dark.

"I take it no one has ever put his mouth here?"

He leaned in and slid the tip of his tongue over her clit for a moment.

"N-No."

"Shameful."

"Is it?"

He smiled as he spread her open and took a long lick, moaning at the taste of her.

"Not this part." He licked her again and again. "The part where no man has tasted how salty-sweet you are. I'm going to make you fly apart, Verity."

He sucked her clit gently, over and over until she breathed in soft little sobs.

And then he stopped. She reached out faster than he'd have thought of her and grabbed his hair, tugging.

"Shh. I'm not done."

Her breathing calmed a little as he watched her again, sliding his middle finger around and around her gate, pushing inside to stretch her. So tight his cock throbbed with want.

"How long?"

"What?"

"How long has it been since you've been fucked?"

"Two years."

He looked up her body as he took another lick. "He died three years ago?"

"Nearly four now. It was . . . doesn't matter. I was lonely. It was forgettable."

He licked again and again, stretching her as he added another finger.

Her muscles froze, tensing as she sucked in a breath.

"Let go. Breathe. Don't tense up." He spoke against her slick flesh as she came, as the taste of her, the sweetness he'd been lapping up, exploded into something else. Spice. Pepper. Heated as her pleasure bloomed on his tongue, against his lips.

He kissed his way up her belly, pausing when he caught sight of the tears on her cheeks and worried he'd pushed her too hard.

"Are you all right?"

"Yes." She opened her eyes. "Yes, yes. It was wonderful. I've just never . . . not that. Not with anyone."

He kissed her cheeks, tasting her tears. She wound her arms around his neck, holding him tight for a moment. And then she pushed him back, kissing his neck, down to the hollow of his throat. The cool silk of her hair slid against his skin like a caress, the scent of it, flowers and sunlight, seemed to dig into his memory with claws. He knew no matter what else happened, he'd never lose this memory.

She kissed across his chest, licking over his nipples and looking up at him. "I never realized men liked this."

He arched when she sucked his nipple and let her teeth slide against it as she let go.

"Can't say for anyone else. But when you do that I surely do like it, yes."

She smiled and went back to it, kissing him, sliding her hands all over his upper body. She licked a line down his belly until she got to his cock, grabbing it and looking at it closely.

"Kiss it."

She did.

Then she licked over it and licked again.

James had forced it on her many times. But this was different. *Loyal* was different. He tasted right. His skin taut and hot to the touch. She held him at the root, licking all the way from the head to her hand. Learning what made him jump, what brought that moan to his lips. What made him hiss with pleasure.

It was delicious to do this with him. It wasn't a requirement. Something she dreaded as a responsibility. She *liked* it. Her sister never said much about her intimate life with her husband, but she had said something once about how she looked forward to their time alone, when she could make him feel better and ease the day from his shoulders.

She hadn't understood it then, having wished daily that James would drink himself unconscious so she could avoid any intimate contact with him.

But she understood it now. Hoped that her sister had this with Emeril.

She licked around the crown of him, delighting in the sounds he made in response. She palmed his sac, pressing the pads of her fingers over the pucker of his ass. His answering groan told her he liked that very much.

She kept him nice and wet, up and down, around the head.

He was rather . . . large. Thick. A tingle of curiosity slid through her belly. Excited at the idea of having him in her, wondering how it would feel. Wanting it very badly.

His fingers had been tangled in her hair, holding loosely, but he shifted, wrapping it around his fist and holding her steady as he thrust into her mouth.

Her skin beaded into gooseflesh. She was wet again, aching to be filled.

And then he stopped with a snarl.

She was about to tell him if he stopped now he'd best sleep with one eye open. But he shifted, sitting up.

"On my lap."

"On top of you?"

He smiled and it sent a slither of want over her skin. "Oh yes. Never had it that way?"

She shook her head.

"Get over here. Straddle my waist. Knees on either side of my body."

She did as he said and realized it would be fine. She'd know what to do.

He grabbed his cock to angle it, sliding that fat head through her pussy. Teasing, she realized.

"Sit when you're ready. If I was on top I'd slam into your cunt hard and fast. But it's been a while and you need to go slow so I don't hurt you. You need to take control because when it comes to you, my control is weak."

What could she say to that? The things he said filled her with emotions she couldn't fully name.

She took him at the root where his hand had been. He moved his grip, one hand at her hip; the other found her nipple and began that tug, tug and roll.

"Mmm, you're so wet."

She would have been embarrassed perhaps if it was another man saying so. But his words weren't meant to shame. They were meant to incite. As he was incited by her.

The power of that built in her belly and she let herself be eased by it.

She began to move down on him. The head of him was thick and fat and she breathed, letting it feel good, letting the worry fall away because he wanted her. She didn't know what would happen in three days when he left, but she knew without a doubt that he wanted what was happening between them right then and it was enough.

He stretched her slowly as she kept taking him inside. The burn at first would dissolve away into pleasure. James had never allowed for that. Had never let any of the pain dissolve and all it was was a burn.

This was what she'd dreamed of with her hand in her drawers late at night in the dark as she lay alone in bed. *This* is what it could be and she would enjoy it without shame.

HE CLENCHED HIS JAW, sweat on his brow, ordering himself to let her set the pace. Trying to ignore the screaming in his head that told him to take her. To slam his cock balls deep into her cunt and then let her adjust.

Instead, he looked at her features as she slid down. Watched the tension slide away as the pleasure took over. Never in all his days had he seen anything even approaching this sort of beauty.

The pleasure he felt was edged with near pain. She was so tight. The hot, wet embrace of her inner walls tortured him as she fluttered all around.

"Okay?"

Her eyelids came up and her gaze cleared. "Yes," she exhaled on a gasp.

And then she began to move. Slow, up and down. And he forced himself to let her do it. To find her pace, to see what she liked.

"There are other ways you can move as well," he said, his lips against the skin of her shoulder.

"How?"

He took her hips and helped her circle, wide and then tight. He showed her a back and forth slide that she seemed to really like given the warm rush of her as she moved.

"Like that."

Her head fell back as she slid herself back and forth, back and forth on him. She ground her clit against him, a ghost of a smile on her lips.

"Yes, like that indeed."

He moved one hand between them, letting his fingers brush against her clit with each movement she made. She gasped, her eyes opening again.

"Embrace it. Let it come and let it feel good."

She nodded, catching her lip between her teeth as she did. He let it go as long as he could before he began to move as well, pushing up as she moved back and forth. Her lips opened and he swallowed the exhalation as he kissed her hard.

"Yes. Do whatever, take it from me. Just"

He did. Took over the pace, using his hand at her hip to continue to help her slide back and forth and he fucked up into her body over and over and over. She ground herself against his fingers, her cunt tightening around him as she turned superheated, as the hot rush of her sweet juices flowed and she exploded, sending him right over in her wake.

She sighed, sated, as he shifted to lay her at his side.

"I can't believe you made me wait years for that, lawman," she mumbled as he pulled her close.

He snorted a laugh.

"Me either, widow."

CHAPTER SIX

SHE WAS PULLED from sleep by the repeated beep of the blip receiver.

She sat up, pushing her hair from her face. She smelled like him. On her hands, on her skin, between her thighs. She smiled as she got from bed as easily as she could, not wanting to wake him.

His eyes snapped open though, as her feet hit the floor.

"What is it?" Totally alert.

"How do you do that?" She pulled her clothes on quickly. He shrugged, his gaze on her as she moved.

"Something important is coming over the blip. I'll be back. I need to go attend to it."

"I'll come with you. You don't need to be out so late, not all alone."

"How do you think I do it when you're not here?" She headed from the room, slipping her feet into her house shoes and grabbing a robe for the warmth.

"Ah, but I *am* here."

She didn't fail to notice the way he grabbed his weapon, sliding it into the belt he strapped on after he got his pants up. Dangerous.

She hustled down the stairs and out into the cool stillness of the pre-dawn hours outside. She unlocked the door to the mail office quickly, heading back, knowing the way, even through the darkness.

Three blips? She picked up the two that had fallen from the collection arm to the floor, handing them to him. Anything being sent at this time using the emergency channel would be something he'd need to see.

He turned on the light and read them quickly, his mouth drawing into a tight, disapproving line. "I need to go to the garrison office with these." He took the one that had just come in when she handed it over. "This one too. You go right back upstairs. If you hear the alarm I want you to go into lockdown, do you understand me?"

"What's happening?"

"Brigands hit Northern Tip. They've been seen just a bit up the road. They attacked an official transport as well."

She shivered. That was all so very close to Silver Cliffs. "All right." She handed him her keys. "You know which one unlocks everything. I'll be waiting for you."

He watched her carefully for long moments, before his gaze went back to the blip receiver.

"I'll run over to the garrison if any more come. Go."

He moved to the door with her but just before she opened up, he pulled her close, his mouth coming down on hers hard and fast. She pushed herself to his body, already getting used to it. Knowing she shouldn't and choosing to ignore that voice.

"I'll be back when I can."

She headed back upstairs, straight for her gun closet. Best to be prepared if things went the direction she feared they might.

HE POUNDED on the door of the garrison and it opened up rather quickly, the gun pointed at his face lowered once he was recognized.

"Blips." He stalked through the door. "Jackson here?"

"He's a'home."

Loyal gave the man a look. "Well go on then and get him. I'm going to rouse my people and we'll all meet back here as soon as possible."

The guard scampered off as Loyal headed down the hill to get the rest of his crew together.

Haldeman took the blips from Loyal's hand, reading them quickly. Loyal gave him credit for the way he simply took it in and formatted a plan.

"We need scouts down by the Highway."

Loyal looked to Trinity where she stood at the ready, near the door. "You go with one of Haldeman's people. Get down there and let me know what you see." He turned back to Jackson. "None better than Trinity."

Jackson nodded. "Good to know. Harmon, you go with Trinity. Take the trails. Stay off the road."

Trinity and Harmon disappeared out the door after Marcus squeezed her hand quickly. The two had been a couple since before they came onto Loyal's team. Some commanders didn't approve of partners on the same road crew. Loyal didn't care one way or the other as long as no personal shit spilled into official business.

And it hadn't, so he had no call going and having feelings one way or the other about it.

"At this stage, we don't know enough to get everyone worked up." Loyal eased back, leaning against the corner of a desk.

"Verity knows about this?" Jackson held up the papers.

"Aye."

But he didn't need to defend her, Jackson merely nodded. "She'll keep it to herself. She takes that seriously. I'm going to raise the watch level in town. We don't need to call a full alert, but people need to be sure they've got plenty of ammunition and some stores set by in case we get ourselves under siege."

Loyal nodded. "We'll postpone the leaving until we know for sure you're safe."

"Glad to have you in town should this happen."

He thought of Verity. He was too.

They stayed, going over the garrison's basic emergency plan, Loyal approving most of it, making suggestions where he saw they might be needed. Jackson Haldeman was a smart man. He'd have made a good lawman if he'd wanted to be.

"You know where I am when you hear back from the scouts. I'm going to send a few blips back to Shelter City."

"I'll be up in a bit."

He headed back up to Verity's place. Noting the lights burned in her windows. He went around back and into the blip office, sending back his official response, filling them in with what he knew for sure. Which at that point wasn't a whole lot.

When he'd gotten back upstairs, she'd made a big breakfast.

"I figured you might be hungry. I'm baking too. May as well lay in some supplies just in case."

He noted she'd lined rifles up at the various windows.

"The shutters are in good shape." Verity waved a hand toward the windows, meaning the siege shutters they'd draw should the garrison be overrun. They had slots for a rifle cut into them. "I just had them checked last harvest. Jackson had the whole garrison do a drill."

"Haldeman is setting the garrison on alert." He poured himself some black tea and she shooed him to the table, filling a plate for him and setting it in front of him.

"He'll be up soon I wager. To check the blips and give me the broadsheets to post."

Her store would be the nerve center for the town's citizens. The garrison was the law enforcement hub, but he knew the townsfolk would come to the mercantile for the news before they'd gather at the garrison offices. She'd post the broadsheets with the instructions for everyone to follow on the boards out front.

"You ever gone through this before?"

"An attack?"

He nodded.

"Once when I was eight or nine we were overrun. It was back before they built the wall to reach the mountains behind us. My parents hid us in the root cellar. They got pretty far into Silver Cliffs. Set fire to buildings near the gates. We've had alerts here and there since."

He stood and went to her, brushing the backs of his fingers against her cheek. "I'm going to protect you."

She nodded. "I know." Utter faith in him shone through her gaze.

"Come sit and eat with me. I'm sure it's going to be a busy day for everyone.

You'll need to eat too."

She did, but before he could talk with her about what had happened between them the night before, Jackson came in and sat with them, eating as he and Loyal went over next steps.

By the time they'd finished, she'd gone down to post the broadsheets and open the mercantile for business.

And then Trinity had come back with news that sent everyone scrambling.

Brigands had been seen gathering on the Highway near the turnoff for Silver Cliffs.

VERITY CONTINUED TO WORK, trying to think on this as just another drill. Trying not to be afraid or to panic. There was no reason to jump into being afraid just yet. They were fairly well prepared. And they had something a lot of garrisons didn't when they were attacked, five lawmen working with the garrison defense.

Her sister came into the mercantile. "We want you to come stay with us until this is over."

Verity shook her head. "I need to be here to monitor the blips and to keep people informed. Do you have enough food and ammunition? Enough fuel?"

They were all advised to keep at least a moon's worth of supplies in case of a prolonged siege but people oftentimes put such things off.

"Jackson can put someone here to monitor the blips after you close. This is silliness. You're not a man. You're not a soldier. You should be protected."

"I'm also not helpless. I'm a better shot than many men in Silver Cliffs. My home is well fortified. I've got a lawman staying in my spare room. I'll be fine. I appreciate the concern, but I'm all right."

"He's not moving to the garrison barracks?" One of Constance's brows slid up and Verity braced herself for the lecture she feared would come.

"They've all decided to keep the lawmen scattered through town as they are now. They have personal communicators so they know if there's a problem. He can run and be down at the barracks in a flash. They all can. No use sleeping on a cot when he can stay here." She shrugged.

"You have anything you want to tell me?"

It wasn't a crime, or even a sin for her to take solace in Loyal's arms if she wanted to. As a widow, she had more freedom than she would have if she'd never married. But some people, maybe even her sister, might look askance.

She had no intention of confessing to her sister as if it was something to be ashamed of.

"Jackson is sweet on you. Is he all right with the lawman staying at your house?"

"I've been owned by a man. Owing him news and explanations of every moment of my day, aye? I will not, ever, owe that to another human being again. Jackson can feel however he wants about where Loyal is staying and it means no nevermind to me, understand?"

Constance sighed, nodding. "They're not all like James. Jackson would be good for you. I'm just saying maybe take how he feels into account."

"I know what you're saying." Verity closed the discussion firmly.

"All right then. Please come to our house if things get scary. I'll feel much better if you do."

"Thank you. I will."

"And Tobin says you've given him the week off until this blows over?"

"Yes. He should be home where he can protect you and the house."

Her sister rolled her eyes. "I want him here in the daytime. He gets under my feet at home. He's disagreeable because he'd rather be here where he can see everything. I know you'll send him home if things change."

"You sure?"

Her sister nodded.

"All right then. The windows need a good cleaning. I'll put him on that so at least he'll be too tired to argue with his daddy when he gets home at night."

Constance laughed. "Thank you." She hugged Verity, kissing her cheek. "You think on what I said." And left before Verity could argue.

CHAPTER SEVEN

PEOPLE HAD TAKEN to congregating there on her large porch, watching the street leading down the hill. Watching the gates and whatever they could beyond them.

She'd done a brisk business over the last two days. A few enterprising souls showed up several times a day with baskets of sandwiches and wrapped bundles of meat and rice or grains, selling them for snacks and luncheon. People found a way, she thought with a smile. Even in the darkest of times, people found a way.

There was a curfew in effect at sunset. She sent people home as she and Tobin pulled the shutters over the windows on the first floor, locking them into place.

"I'll see you tomorrow. Go on home and take that bundle to your mother. I made her some of the tea she likes. It'll settle her system."

Her sister tended to be violently ill in the early months of her pregnancies. Luckily, the combination of herbs and flowers Verity dried for her tea seemed to aid and ease her sister's discomfort. It was nice to be needed. Nice to be able to help.

Tobin nodded, kissing her cheek and running off home, the bundle under his arm. Loyal hadn't been around the night before as he'd done whatever they did down the garrison offices. But he came in as she stood in her kitchen wondering if she should take some dinner down to them all.

He held up a basket. "Went fishing today since we were out scouting anyway. I even cleaned them for you."

"This is a division of labor I'm quite happy with." She smiled with a wink, taking the basket.

"Have I actually found something you aren't good at?"

"Gutting fish and scraping off the skin and scales?" She wrinkled her nose. "One does what one must. But if I can avoid such tasks, I'm pleased to do so."

He shrugged, a smile on his lips. "What'll you give me then if I do all the fish gutting and scaling?"

She put the basket on the counter and moved to him. "Whatever you want."

He licked his lips and she let the power roll through her. The ability to turn his head and keep his attention. The ability to make his cock swell and his mouth turn up into a rather wicked grin.

"Why don't you get on your knees. To get started."

She did, obeying immediately, looking up his body into his face. "Let me check the door."

She grabbed the waist of his trousers, opening them quickly, pulling his cock out, hot and hard in her grip. She licked over the head, tasting the spice of his seed.

"You worried someone might come up and see me here, on my knees, your cock in my mouth?"

She had no idea where the words had come from. She'd thought such filthy things before, but never had she said them aloud.

He shivered, rooted to the spot. "Go on then." He rolled his hips as she put her mouth around the head, pressing in deeper and pulling back.

He undid her hair, his fingers sifting through it over and over as she fell under that rhythmic touch. Until he wrapped it around his fist and held her exactly where he wanted her.

At first he'd tried to tell himself he wouldn't do this again. But he'd been a liar because he'd been dreaming of this since he'd pulled out of her cunt the night before last.

The reality of this woman on her knees before him, that sweet mouth wrapped around his cock, her hair around his fist as he fucked her face was better than anything he'd ever dreamed.

"Breathe through your nose. Slow and steady." He nearly crooned the words, sliding his free hand over her head, down to caress her cheek even as he kept thrusting into that mouth.

"Can you take more? Hm?"

She whimpered, but not in fear. He had to close his eyes a moment at the way the sound affected him.

"I think you can. For me." He thrust harder, she hummed her pleasure and the sound vibrated up his cock, into his gut.

"I'm going to come in your mouth. And every time I look at you I'm going to know that. And you will too."

She dragged her nails lightly over his balls and he groaned, unable to tear his gaze from her, from the sight of his cock sliding into her mouth and coming back out, wet and dark.

He heard her breathe through her nose, deeply like he'd told her. Orgasm began to dig its nails into him as he watched her swallow his cock again and again.

He fought the urge to close his eyes when it hit, instead he watched as her lids closed, as she flushed a pretty pink when he came. She didn't let go either. Not until *she* was ready to be done.

And then when she let him pull back, she looked up and licked her lips.

He'd given life to this more carnal Verity. He saw glimpses of it here and there since that first night. Knowing no one else had noticed. No one but him. She seemed to ooze sensuality now.

And he let himself be fascinated by it. Later he'd have to deal with it, but for the time he was there, he'd soak it in.

He helped her up, kissing her hard.

"After dinner I'm going to feast on your cunt until you have to scream into the pillow. And then I'm going to fuck you so hard your breasts bounce."

She licked her lips again and swallowed, nodding.

"Yes. Please."

SHE MOVED around the kitchen on shaky legs as she put a meal together. He sat at the table, reading, making notes and watching her with covetous eyes. He made her knees wobble.

"So any new sightings?"

He looked up. "Nothing new. They're good at blending in. Not always so dependent on vehicles, which means they don't need the roads."

"Are you still leaving tomorrow?"

She hoped not.

"Most likely no. One of the blips today advised us to stay in place."

"You should take me then. When you leave I mean." Now that she'd blurted it out she felt better. Lighter.

She turned the fish in the pan, tipping to get the oils so she could spoon them over the sweet flesh a few times.

"We've talked about this."

"No we haven't. You'd said I was better off here than traveling out there. I want to see the world. I want to know what it's like outside these walls. I've lived here my entire life. I've never been further than half a day's walk from Silver Cliffs. You've been up and down the Highway. You've seen how people live, you've eaten what they eat. You've seen how they dress. I know enough to know it's not all how we are here. I know people do things differently in other places. I want that. I want to see it."

"You want to leave here where the walls keep you safe from the brigands?" His gaze seemed to burn through her as she stirred the rice, fluffing it and putting it into a bowl she placed on the table.

"You're alive. The people you travel with are alive. The people who drive the transports are alive. Don't patronize me."

"I'm not patronizing you. I'm telling you it's safe here. You're better off here. The world outside will change you. I don't want that. Can't you see?"

"Why is it about what you want anyway? What about what I want?"

"And then what? Hm? You leave here to do what? Go where? With who?"

She rolled her eyes and put the bread, still warm from the oven, on the table. "Please pour us some juice."

He sighed, getting up to do so.

"With you, of course. Trinity and Marcus drive together."

"They're lawmen. You're a shopkeeper."

That hurt. He was right, of course, which didn't really negate the hurt.

"If you don't want me along, just say so."

He started to speak but a knock on the door interrupted them both. "Don't think I can't see the relief on your face. This isn't over."

He walked past her, pausing to give her a hard, quick kiss before he moved to the door, letting Jackson in.

"Trackers just came back. Brigands are about two miles down. They're sticking close to the river. But they're headed this way."

"I'll make this portable." She moved to sandwich the fish in the center of the crusty roll along with some of the pickle. "Jackson, would you like one?" She held up the bread after she'd wrapped it and placed it on Loyal's empty plate.

"Aye, that would be mighty fine, Verity. Much appreciated."

His eyes took her in, pausing at her mouth and then shifting over to Loyal briefly.

Loyal disappeared into his room and came back out with a leather roll, which he unfurled on the tabletop. He slid into an overvest, one she knew would repel bullets and blades. His gaze had gone flat and hard, his mouth set in a line.

She handed a sandwich to Jackson and he ate it as he watched Loyal take the weapons in the roll and strap them on.

Blades, guns, he tucked a few magazines for his weapons in a pocket of his trousers.

"I need to get to my people. Take the town up from general alert to full alert. I want everything locked down."

Jackson nodded as he ate. "Done. I'll send runners out." He turned to Verity. "Thank you for the dinner. I hadn't realized how hungry I was." He smiled, reaching out to brush some crumbs from her skirt. "You lock down too. Are you going to head to your sister's?"

She shook her head. "No. James let you all use the house the last time we had an incursion. He sure told the story often enough. You can see plenty from the attic and the roof." She took a key from a nearby drawer. "This unlocks the store and the stairs. Consider this my permission to use the roof and attic for your men as well."

"Don't go doing anything stupid, you hear me, Verity?" He took her hands. "You see them coming and you get yourself locked in your cellar. I know you have an exit from there to the pasture out back. You get gone if you need to."

She nodded. "I have supplies hidden out there. I'll be fine." He paused as if he were going to speak, but Loyal cleared his throat as he kept arming himself, though he kept his gaze down on what he was doing.

"I'll check in on you later." Jackson headed to the door and looked to Loyal before leaving. "I'll see you at the garrison shortly."

And was gone.

She moved to Loyal, bending to tie the laces on his boots. He hauled her to her feet when she'd finished. His gaze severe, hard. "You *will* remain here in this house, do you understand me? Green flare if you need to evacuate. You see two greens and you get that pretty little ass downstairs and into that cellar. Use the full locks and the big heavy door. You get yourself gone. I'll find you when it's safe."

"I'm not stupid. I won't stay if we get overrun."

"Nay, not stupid. But passionate." He sighed. "They will . . . they will savage every female in this garrison if they catch them. I don't want that to happen to you. Or to anyone here." He amended, but it was late enough that she knew he cared about her in a way he wasn't sure how to process. Which was good as she felt quite the same.

"I have no desire to be savaged. Though, should a certain lawman want to pillage?" She raised her brow and smiled. He shook his head.

"You're a handful, Verity Coleman."

"I am. Don't forget it."

He hauled her against him, the blades, though sheathed, pressing into her flesh through her clothes. A reminder of what else he was. It thrilled her though she knew it was dangerous.

His kiss wasn't safe. It was hard and fast, a gnash of teeth, the nip of her bottom lip. He branded her with that kiss. "Your lips are still swollen from my cock," he spoke against her mouth at last. "Haldeman noticed that."

"Yes." She tried not to pant, but it was difficult.

"Mine." He kissed her hard one last time and stepped back. "Watch out the window. Keep the lights off. Lock this place down and do not come out unless you get the signal or are escorted by one of us or Haldeman's men. Promise."

She nodded.

He grabbed two rifles and headed out. She went down, checked the locks on the windows and pulled the heavy plates down, covering the doors and windows. She slid the bolts and locks into place and headed back upstairs, doing the same on the main door from the back stairs. She'd keep the exit down the back stairs, up to the attic, down to the cellar and her tunnel to escape locked, but accessible. The lights went off all over town as the runners spread out. Shutters clanked shut, locks clicked out through the night.

She only hoped they were ready to repel the assault she knew in her bones was coming.

HE GATHERED HIS TEAM, who'd already been on alert and were all ready.

"They had a group of about twenty that I could see." Indigo indicated a map on the table nearby and they moved over.

Haldeman and several of his men were there as well, watching, ready for orders. In a situation like this one, Loyal would be the commanding officer.

"They were here." Indigo pointed.

"There's a trail just ahead." Haldeman drew a line from the river toward the garrison. "It would take them around the bridge, but they'd still have to cross the river. Right now it's swollen with melting snow-pack. Several feet above the normal levels. And brutally cold. Too cold to swim across and live."

"Other than the main bridge, where else can they cross safely?"

"Nearer the pass." Haldeman pointed miles east of the garrison, higher up in the mountains. "There's a bridge up that way. They can cross there. Even if they ran it would take them an extra day, day and a half. The climb is brutal. Maybe it'll discourage them."

"Depends on the why of this attack." Stace looked over the map. "I can get to the bridge up on the pass. Blow it so they can't cross."

"What do you mean depends on the why?" One of Haldeman's men stood forward.

Trinity shrugged. "You can't count on the brigands to do things how you might. They don't think like we do. If they're hungry or angry at having to walk extra they may not give up like you or I might. Go pick an easier target. No, they might figure the extra work is worth whatever you got in these walls. Or they may be so mad that they see this as revenge for making them work so hard. Or maybe they're starving and they'll come no matter what. They don't think like regular folk is what I'm saying. They're brigands. Closer to animal than people at times, 'specially times like these when they're on a hunt."

Trinity knew them well. Her family had been taken by them. She'd been raised as a camp slave for several years until she'd escaped. Just ten years old, she'd leapt off a moving brigand vehicle and into the road in the path of a lawman's escort. It was lucky they hadn't shot her but stopped to help. Against regulations to do such things, but it had saved her life and she'd been with the lawmen ever since.

"I'm going to advise you let Stace blow that bridge."

"It's a way for us to hunt without having to go all the way around."

"I understand that. But if you can slow down a gang of brigands that's going to be better than having to deal with rebuilding it when it's warmer. You see my meaning? We may not be here the next time. You blow that bridge and they have no other choice but to come over the main bridge. It cuts down their avenue of attack. Makes it manageable."

Haldeman sent a hand through his hair and then nodded. "Go on. Tell me what you need and how many you want to come with you."

CHAPTER EIGHT

HE SHUFFLED BACK up the hill some hours later. He'd been up for far longer than he should have been and Indigo, his second, had shoved him out the door with orders to get some kip and a meal before he came back.

It was the calm before the storm. They'd prepared all they could for the time being. The team had left to destroy the bridge at the upper river with several of the garrison's best trackers so he had every reason to believe they'd finish the job and likely be back at the garrison before the brigands had even reached that far.

His people would also do a survey of the river to be sure there were no weak spots to get across. They could use boats to get across, but the current was fast as well as cold. And the brigands were many things, but sophisticated they weren't.

There was nothing to do at that point but rest while they could so he'd nodded and left.

The shutters were locked all over town, though some were out and about doing necessary business. But the mercantile was closed, he was pleased to see.

He went around back, unlocking the large blast doors covering the entrance and sliding them back into place when he'd finished.

She was curled in a chair near a shuttered window. He smiled at the juxtaposition of her there, small, the tumble of hair making her seem even smaller, and the rifles at each window.

He'd only gotten three steps into the room before she awoke.

"News?" She stood, stretching, and before he could think to say anything he was on her, his mouth on hers, his hands pulling her close. He *needed* that contact in a way that should have scared him. Most likely would later.

After.

He shoved her hair back over her shoulder one handed and slid the robe she'd been wearing off her shoulders, leaving her in a long night-dress that buttoned all the way up the front. He couldn't wait. Didn't want to wait. He grabbed either side and tugged hard, the material parting on the sound of buttons flying.

She gasped and he paused, waiting for rebuke, but got none. Instead she moaned, arching into his touch as he slid covetous hands over her bare skin. He'd had this well of need for her that appeared bottomless. And since the first kiss, he'd been unable to resist her.

She offered herself to him and he had no ability to turn away.

Pale and beautiful in the dim light that made its way through the shutters, he took her in as she stood, bare, the remains of her clothing pooled at her feet.

He fell to his knees. "I believe, before we were so unfortunately interrupted by brigand talk, I had plans for you." He leaned in to kiss her belly, below her navel. "For

She shivered, sliding her fingers through his hair.

It was cool in the house and he noted the gooseflesh. "Wait for me there." He pointed at the settee, before he moved to the woodstove and built the fire within up. The air began to warm a little and he moved back to where she sat, watching him without a word.

He took her mouth, still on his knees. She wrapped her legs around his body, holding him close.

"So beautiful," he murmured, kissing down her neck to her breasts, licking and biting her nipples until she made a whimper deep in her throat. "I've been thinking about the way you taste all night."

HE'D COME in looking haunted.

Long and lean, his hair close cropped so she could see the lines of his face. The lips, currently cruising down her ribcage, the blades of his cheekbones, the blue-gray eyes that failed to miss anything. He'd come in, loaded down, she knew, with the worries and fears of everyone in Silver Cliffs.

He'd stood looking at her as she'd shaken off her fitful sleep and managed to stand, moving to him as if he drew her by some magic.

But it wasn't magic, it was him. Her heart beat for him. Had for years now, she realized.

Big, strong hands slid down her torso and to her hips. He continued to kiss down her body until he got to her pussy and she shivered. Not from cold. From the sheer delight she knew she was about to enjoy.

"Sit back."

She did, obeying, watching down her body as he pushed her thighs open and spread her with his thumbs.

The room had warmed since he'd built the fire up, but his hands on her built the fire in her belly. His gaze found hers, locked as he kissed her knee and then up her thigh. He kissed her there, the heart of her, like it was her mouth. Fascinated, she kept watch, seeing his tongue lap, flick, taste her in such an intimate way it nearly sliced through her. No one had been this close to her and he reveled in it. She reveled in the way he touched her. Like he couldn't get enough.

This man of few words but for the occasional whispered dirty ones between them in the dim. He was thrilling. Exciting. Fearsome and not just because he was a walking weapon. But because he made her want things she knew she shouldn't. And did anyway.

Climax curled her toes, swept up her calves and thighs and burst over her until she indeed had to scream out, her face in a pillow from the settee should anyone be out on the street.

He stood. "Face the back of the settee. On your knees. Brace yourself with your hands."

Still shaking from orgasm, she rose up and did as he'd said, the thrill of whatever he'd planned washing through her. He moved behind her, the heat of his body against hers after he'd gotten rid of his trousers.

The head of his cock brushed against her and slid in easily as he grunted. "So wet."

She pushed back against him, her face burning with a blush. But not of shame. He never made her feel that for what they did together.

He set a pace, fast, deep. She held on as the settee moved just a little bit as he thrust.

"Want of you has set me on fire," he murmured against the skin of her shoulder. "This is what I think about. Your sweet, hot, wet cunt wrapped around my cock like a fist."

She stuttered a breath, curving her back to take him deeper.

Normally a chatterer, she found herself stunned silent by the things he said when it was just them, when it was this. Skin to skin, his body in hers. His hands caressing every part of her he could reach.

"Yes," she whispered.

"Mine," he whispered back, and she wanted to laugh. Yes, yes she was.

Instead she nodded quickly. "Yours."

That seemed to satisfy him for a time as he continued to thrust. His teeth dug into the flesh of her shoulder as he groaned. The pain silvered into something else, something pleasurable as she felt the jerk of his cock deep within her, as she knew she made him feel this way. *Her.*

She smiled against the fabric of the settee, the nub of it against her inflamed skin.

"Let us nap for a time." He stood back and picked her up, walking her not into his room, but hers. He pulled the blankets back and she moved over, giving him room to follow. Which he did.

She moved into the hollow where his arm met his body, resting her head there. His arms surrounded her and she closed her eyes. Satisfied and unafraid.

HE AWOKE to the scent of coffee and fried meat.

She spoke in low tones to someone, which is what brought him to his feet and into his pants. He had nowhere to come out but through her bedroom door and realized he wanted to be seen. Wanted whoever it was to know she was his.

He froze, his hand on the knob. *Stupid.* Stupid to think in those terms. But there it was. He still tasted her, smelled her on his skin and he wasn't ready to give that up. Wasn't ready to give *her* up.

He'd lived through a lot. Survived the loss of his family, years on the Highway. Battles. He brushed a hand over his belly, against the ridges of the scars he bore from a nasty ambush that nearly ended with his death.

He'd driven up the Highway, seen the silvery gray cliffs rising up to the east and his heart had eased. Had eased because he knew he'd be seeing her soon. Knew he'd be in her parlor, listening to her voice as she told him about all the silly goings on in Silver Cliffs. Eating the meals she'd created. Sleeping with such beauty and perfection only on the other side of the wall and it had been enough.

Barely enough, but enough.

But it wasn't anymore. Now that he'd loosed the tide of desire that had lay within him for so long there was no going back. He couldn't drive back through those gates and not come to her. Not seek the solace of her lips, the sweetness of her touch.

He was sure his shirt was tucked in before he opened the door to find Indigo leaning against a counter in the kitchen, watching her as she cooked.

Verity looked up from where she worked, a smile on her face when she saw him. "I hope you're hungry. Indigo just arrived to fill you in on what's going on."

"My timing, as usual, is impeccable as I was also invited to stay and share the meal." Indigo flashed very white teeth as he smiled at Verity.

She blushed, patting his arm as she passed.

"You can wash up. I'm just about to get everything on the table."

Indigo tipped his chin. "Yes, ma'am. Thank you." He moved past her toward the bathroom where he shot Loyal a smug look. Loyal barely resisted rolling his eyes.

He moved to her, kissing her quickly. "Smells good."

"Comes in handy when folks in town pay me with food and I've got a hungry lawman under my roof."

Hungry, yes. And not just for food.

"I'm sorry we've been invaded." He spoke quietly, standing close enough to smell her skin.

She shrugged with a small, satisfied smile as she began to put platters on the table. He moved around her, adding plates and utensils.

"It's all right. I like him and I like that because he's here, you have the opportunity to take some downtime to eat and get a meal into your belly."

Indigo came back out and they sat, digging in, the silence only broken by the sounds of utensils on plates. Finally, once they'd had a chance to fill up a little, Indigo sipped a mug of tea and looked over to Loyal, his gaze quickly cutting to Verity and back.

"Go ahead. You can speak freely."

"Bridge is destroyed. We left someone in place up at the pass to report back when the brigands arrived. Not back yet though."

"It's a goodly hike up that far. Should take a fair bit of time." She said this as she refilled everyone's glass.

"I'm not alarmed. Yet. Haldeman would have said if he was worried."

"So you mean to put them on the only possible path? Across the main bridge. Easier to defend that way I suppose. I read about it once in an ancient military manual. Killbox?"

Indigo sent Loyal a raised brow for a moment. "That's it, indeed. Smart as well as pretty and a mighty fine cook too. No wonder Loyal is always fussy when we have to leave."

She smiled, but said nothing else.

"We've got scouts out, keeping an eye on the road and the established trails."

"Is there a chance that they'll get up to the bridge and when they see they can't cross they'll move on?"

"They're unpredictable. It could happen that way. But I don't think it will. I think they'll come because they'll be angry they were thwarted. Because they want this town and whatever is inside it. Because that's who they are."

"Like an animal who tastes human flesh."

Indigo looked back her way. "How's that?"

"We get big cats round here from time to time. Mainly they try to steal livestock. But every once in a while, someone is attacked and it changes the cat. Makes them unpredictable I guess is a good word. As if taking that step somehow changes them and they can't go back. They have to be killed or they'll always be a threat."

He supposed that was a mighty fine metaphor.

"It's like their purpose is to raid. We can't even take them prisoner. They mutilate themselves while in custody. Try to kill everyone in sight. They'll kill themselves if they can." Indigo's gaze went distant, as if he was remembering. They all had memories.

She looked away, giving him that space, busying herself. "I think I'll make some sandwiches for you to take back to the garrison. I imagine people might be in need of some food."

Indigo got to his feet. "I'll take it over if you like. We don't need you yet," he spoke over his shoulder to Loyal.

Who stood. No matter how much he wanted to crawl back into bed with her, he had a job to do. Keeping Silver Cliffs safe meant keeping her safe. And that's what mattered.

"Go ahead on. I'll be over in a bit. I want to check on the blips and then I'll bring the food over."

Indigo stood, nodded and turned to Verity. "Thank you for the meal."

She took his hands. "It must be hard sometimes. All the traveling you do. Sometimes nothing is better than to enjoy a home cooked meal. You're welcome at my table any time."

Indigo ducked his head, charmed, it was plain to see. "Much appreciated, ma'am."

She smiled, so pretty. "I'm younger than you are I'd wager. So how about you call me Verity instead of ma'am?"

"All right then. Lock up and stay safe. I expect you know how to use those?" He tipped his chin toward the rifles.

"I do. I've even been doing a lot of target practice lately. Making myself better."

"Good."

A few more instructions from Loyal and he'd gone quickly, leaving quiet in his wake.

Loyal moved to her, pulling her close. "I'm sorry to eat and run off."

She shook her head. "You have a job to do. I understand that. People need you and your leadership."

He blew out a breath, nervous to be held up as an example like that. Knowing the whys of course—it was his job—and lawmen were important in their culture. Looked to for leadership. He would do it because that was what he was bred to do. And he'd hope he didn't let anyone down in the process.

"Go and wash up. I'll come down to the garrison with you with the food."

"I need this first." He dipped down to kiss her long and slow. All his angst and worry smoothed out as her taste took over. She sighed into his mouth and he took it, greedy for all of her he could have.

He should have broken the kiss several times, but he kept on, her lips curving up into a smile against his when he finally stepped back. "I really don't want to leave."

She laughed. "Yes you do. I can see you already starting to think on the garrison defenses again. I'm not going anywhere. I'll be here when your day is done and they send you back here to rest."

HE THOUGHT about her words as they walked down the hill to the garrison barracks. He'd never had that before. A woman waiting when his day was done. *Anyone* waiting when his day was done.

Roots.

He'd grown up poor, without too many and then his family had been taken from him in a violent act. At fifteen he was thrust into the military and had gravitated to the lawmen because it had been solitary. He drove in his vehicle in a team, yes, but alone too.

It had suited him for a long time. The life without roots. But mainly it was that he did something worth doing that kept him getting back into his seat each time. He was needed. Necessary. He kept people safe, kept commerce moving. He'd been told plenty of times in his life that he was worthless. But each time they drove through the gates of a garrison town he proved his father wrong.

Jackson's eyes lit when he caught sight of her as they came through the doors some time later. She smiled back, holding up her basket. "I brought some food. Figured you all might need something to get you through the day."

They all set on her, though, Loyal noted, they were orderly. No one pushed and every single person said thank you. She seemed to evoke that.

Stace came in with some others just as she was packing up to leave. "They've turned back and are headed to the main bridge. They tried to burn the brush and tree cover on their side of the river but it's too wet to catch."

She turned and nodded. "I'll be getting back home. Jackson, I'll be up on my roof keeping an eye. I'll let you know if I see anything."

"No you won't. You need to stay inside."

She gave Haldeman a raised brow. "It's my house and my roof and heaven knows I'm safe there. No one can get to me. Especially from the other side of the bridge. They won't even be able to see me. But I have field glasses and I'll see them." She gave Haldeman her back, which was good because Loyal caught the annoyance on the other man's face.

Verity Coleman wasn't a female to be managed. Strong. With a mind of her own and if she wanted up on her roof she'd go there. Best to urge her to keep back and report anything she saw than to go forbidding her from something she was going to do no matter what.

"Stay back. They can't reach you from the other side of the bridge, but we don't want them getting any ideas as to strategic points to take either." Loyal escorted her to the door.

She smiled. "Of course. I'll send Tobin with any news."

And she was gone with a swish of skirts.

CHAPTER NINE

YOU WANT to tell me what is going on with the lawman?" Tobin settled in next to her on her roof. She scanned the area with her field glasses.

"What do you mean?"

"You're more a friend than an aunt, really, Verity. I can see the way you look at him. Have looked at him for years. And the way he looks at you. The energy between you two has changed. Even my mother has noticed. He's . . . what do you think is next?"

She thought about it. Thought about telling him to mind his own business. She couldn't really talk to her sister. She loved Constance, but Constance would only tell her Jackson was a better match and the lawman's lifestyle was unsuitable for her.

And her sister would be right in a lot of ways.

"I'm in love with Loyal. I have been for at least a year. We've gotten closer lately." She sipped some water and kept her scan up.

"I don't know how he feels for me. Not precisely. I know he cares about me."

"You want to leave Silver Cliffs, don't you?"

She swallowed back her automatic rejection of the idea.

"I want to see the world outside the gates. I want to hear other accents, see how people live elsewhere. There's so much outside and I haven't seen most of it."

"Do you want him because he's your ticket out? Or because you want him?"

"I've been saving up for several annum now to get on the list to travel to Shelter City. Since before James was killed. I'm going whether I do it with Loyal or not. I don't know that I'd go forever. But . . . I am dying here. Slowly dying." She put the glasses down and turned to Tobin. "My heart aches to know. To learn. To see. And I can't. Not here. Do you see?"

He took her hand, squeezing it for a moment. "I do."

"I want him to take me with him. I know lawmen have lives. Families even. I wouldn't have babies out on the road. I don't think that would be fair, or easy. But Marcus and Trinity travel together."

"She's a lawman too."

"Yes, I know. I know all of this. I want to be with him. Before, when he left I was sad. But now? Now that things are different between us? It tears part of me away when he talks of leaving. I never had this before. If James had left for moons at a time I'd have rejoiced. I like being with Loyal. He makes me happy."

"Probably because you do all the talking." Tobin winked with a grin. She laughed.

"A plus of a taciturn man, Tobin, for a chatty woman. He says what he needs to say, but he doesn't waste anything. Not words, not movement. He's economical, but in the best sort of way."

"Dangerous world out there."

"Yes. But it's not always so. Most of the time they escort the official transport without incident."

"My mother is going to fight you on leaving."

She nodded, picking up the glasses again to scan the path on the other side of the river. "Aye. She will."

"She's not curious."

"She thinks curiosity is dangerous. It's how we were raised."

"I'm on your side."

Tobin settled back, picking up his own field glasses.

"Thank you."

"Will you support me then? When I tell them I want to be a lawman?"

She turned to him, not entirely surprised. "Is that what you really want?"

"I sent in papers, two visits ago, to apply to the training school."

And he'd said nothing. She nodded, reaching out to squeeze his hand. "Then yes, I'll support you. I can talk to Loyal if you like, see if he'll share what it's like."

"He has. I mean, mainly I've spoken to Trinity because she's a tracker and that's what I want to do. I'd have to go to their academy. It's a bit of money to get there. I'm saving for it."

He was one surprise after another.

"I can help you. I have credits set by."

"You do. But for your trip to Shelter City."

"I can do that too. So I have to wait longer." She shrugged. "This is more important. We'll make it happen for you one way or another."

"They won't like it. My parents."

"Probably not. It's not a safe or easy life. They'll want that for you."

"As if it's an easy life here? Behind a plow or whatever I'd find a place doing?"

"You could enter service at the garrison. They've always a need of strong soldiers here."

She wanted to be careful. She loved Tobin and wanted him to be happy, but at the same time, she wanted him to be safe too. Wanted him to make choices that would keep him that way. And without a doubt her sister would blame her for this turn of events.

"I could. I may still. It's an option after academy. I just don't want to be trapped here. I want options. Is it so wrong to want that?"

She shook her head. "No it isn't. You have every right to want that. Every right to pursue a life of your own choosing."

"Sometimes it feels like wanting that is selfish."

She shrugged. "Maybe it is. But if you can't be selfish about creating your own future, what can you be selfish about?"

He was silent for a while as he thought. "Is that what you're doing?"

"My parents traded me like livestock to a man more than twice my age when I was fourteen. I never had a life of my own choosing. Ever. The only freedom I did have was in my imagination. On the page of a book. After he was killed I had a sort of freedom I'd never had before. If it makes me selfish now to want to leave this and see what's out there? If I choose to come back here for good, so be it. I'm capable of more than having babies and wiping down counters in a general store. I may *choose* that in the future. It's not a bad life. I'm not saying that. I'm saying I want to know. I want my choice to be made with more information."

SHE'D BEEN SCANNING the trail and saw movement. Verity leaned forward, peering carefully, noting the shiver of some bushes. Moments later the brigands emerged and marched in the open.

"Tobin, go. Run down to the garrison and tell them I've sighted the brigands near the big tree."

He got up and scampered away without argument and she kept watch.

Moments later it wasn't Tobin who returned, but Loyal. "Where?"

She handed the field glasses over and guided him to the spot, which wasn't hard as a whole band of them had emerged from the treeline.

They were fearsome. A shiver worked through her at the sight. The night was chilly, but they wore little more than some animal skins about their waists. The light of the waning moon, giving way to early morning lit them with purple-blue light. Their faces had been painted, or maybe marked with inks and tattoos.

"Their teeth are filed so they can tear into people when they attack."

She'd heard but had hoped it was rumor.

He turned to her and saw Tobin standing behind. "Go back to the garrison barracks. Tell them two score and five. They've got the usual weapons. I want full lights on that bridge and the sentry fires set immediately."

Tobin raced off.

"What next?"

"The sentry fires will be set along the walls. That'll let them know you see them."

"Obviously we can because they're standing out in the open!"

He turned, taking her hands. "I'm not going to let anything harm you."

She swallowed her fear back. There were twenty-five of them and at least five hundred fighters, more if everyone took up arms who had them and could use them. She could use a weapon. She was all right. They'd be all right.

He caressed her face. "I'd never let anything happen to you. I swear it."

Loyal Alsbaugh wasn't the kind of man she expected sweet words from, though certainly he said lovely things to her from time to time. But he made her feel safe. In a world like theirs, it meant everything to feel that way.

"You're not helpless. Even if I wasn't here, you'd be safe." He paused for several long beats. "But I'm grateful I am. If I'd been elsewhere and got the news, if I hadn't been here knowing you were under siege?" He swallowed and she stood, held by his words, the breeze sending her skirts swaying around her legs, catching a stray curl and bouncing it from her cheek. She could smell his skin. Woodsmoke and gun oil.

The sun was up somewhere, not quite there yet. But the promise of it lightened the sky and she looked up, caught by the masculine lines of his features.

"I'm grateful you are too."

He brushed his lips against hers. "I'm going to send someone up here to keep watch. I want you back inside. Please," he added after she'd given him a look.

"Can I be of help anywhere else?"

He chewed his lip for a time and sighed, deciding to just be blunt. "If you're safe in your house I'll be able to work better. I'll worry if you're out anywhere. I need to focus and gods help me, you're on my mind so much as it is."

The fierce look she'd been wearing softened. The fear and anxiety were gone, replaced by a smile that shot straight to his gut.

But she didn't push it. She nodded.

He escorted her back and resisted re-checking her weapons. He'd already done so when she hadn't been watching.

"You know all the warnings. If there's any emergency communication, use the whistle and we'll send a runner. I don't think they're going to get over the bridge. But it's best to be smart and prepared."

She nodded again. He pulled her close, kissing her until she lost all the stiffness in her spine. Until he throbbed with each heartbeat with the need to take her to the floor and fuck her senseless.

No time for it though.

He tore his mouth away. "I have to go."

She followed him to the door. "Don't get hurt or I'll be vexed."

He grinned and jogged away.

· · ·

HE WAS PLEASED to see his orders being carried out; the sentry torches lined the entire wall surrounding the garrison and could be seen from the highway.

"You think that's it?" Haldeman tipped his head toward the bridge where the brigands had begun to gather.

"I wouldn't count on it. They can travel in bands of several hundred. They often send out smaller raiding parties to reconnoiter the prey." He'd sent out three scouts to see if there were others hidden elsewhere on the way up to the garrison and expected them to report back soon. If they had indications there was a large gathering of brigands he'd put in a blip and send for soldiers from Table Mount.

Otherwise, they'd be expected to repel the offensive force themselves. It wasn't expedient or even possible to have the central government in Shelter City ride out to protect the garrisons outside the main security zone surrounding it. It was simply an accepted fact that the cost of independence for those who lived outside that safest zone was the necessity to protect themselves when they were threatened by outside forces.

"So do we tell them to back off or what?"

"They won't make an immediate attack. They're going to make a camp right out there on the other side of the bridge. So you can see them. It's part of what they do. Build up your dread and terror."

"We have sharp shooters. Let's kill them all and be done. Why are we so afraid of a bunch of animals?" One of the garrison soldiers shrugged a shoulder.

"You'll find that they're close enough for you to see, but just out of range for that. They're feral, yes, but they understand strategy. Don't underestimate them. They live this way. For generations this is how they have survived. Understand that."

"So what do we do then?"

"You need a show of force. Put men up on the sentry points in full view. With weapons. They'll respond to that. You make yourselves a poor target. Show them you can fight back. That you have excellent defenses and will repel an attack. They'll watch you, see how you react. Hold steady and if you're lucky, they'll leave. If they make a move we will react fiercely and immediately. You have to kill them. All of them. Your reaction is what will gauge whether or not they come back. And how soon."

CHAPTER TEN

HE TOOK reports from his scouts. It appeared a smaller party of brigands were down on the highway. Which meant they were waiting to see what happened up at Silver Cliffs before they moved.

It was his hope that they could get out of this without a breach of the bridge. Underlining just how strong Silver Cliffs was. Then the brigands would find another, weaker target.

He convinced Jackson to have some of the businesses open during the day for the residents of Silver Cliffs. He wanted to keep a sense of normalcy, though also on heightened alert. Keeping the residents emotionally well adjusted was key. A long siege could make people more prone to rash decisions, which put everyone at risk. So he wanted them out in their fields and doing their daily tasks to stave that off.

He put everyone on three shifts so that the wall would constantly have soldiers on it and after a long day, he walked back up the hill to Verity's place. He'd eat and rest a while before heading back. Brigands tended to move at night. He didn't think it would be that day, but likely the following if they moved at all. But there was no harm in being prepared.

Earlier that day he'd gone through Silver Cliffs to patrol. He'd wanted to be seen by people, to reassure them they were safe.

Verity had her mercantile open, Tobin at her side as she filled orders and chatted with her customers.

He wanted her.

Wanted to stride up to her, pull her in for a kiss so everyone in the place knew she was his. She'd looked up and smiled, waving. He'd tipped his hat and kept walking.

He'd realized at that moment that it wasn't so much that he planned to hide his involvement with her. Many people in Silver Cliffs had already figured it out. But he had a job and she had hers. He respected her, and considering the bits and pieces he knew about her husband, he realized that sort of possessiveness might not be welcome.

But now the streets were quiet. A sense of expectation hung in the air, but not as fervently fearful as it had been even the day before. He'd often found that once people knew what to expect they were less prone to panic. The show of force and the confident way the garrison defenses had been conducting themselves had given people a sense of direction and safety.

He headed up her back stairs, locking up again in his wake. He smelled something savory, but didn't hear her. Had she taken a nap? He smiled, imagining how he'd wake her up.

Then he heard the water and her voice as she sang. Not as pretty as the rest of her. Verity Coleman was incredibly talented at a lot of things, but those things didn't include singing.

Once he was sure they were alone and he'd locked up and taken a look out toward the gate to be sure things were still quiet, he headed to her, discarding his clothing as he did.

He knocked, not wanting to startle her as he opened up. She smiled when she saw him.

"Why good evening to you, lawman."

"Howdy, ma'am. May I be of some service?"

She took a leisurely look from his toes up to his face, a smile on her lips. "I can think of a great many services I'd be eager for you to provide."

Something about her always eased the knots in his belly. He let himself be happy as she got to her knees and he moved closer.

"Do you need a back scrub?" she asked as he got into the tub, settling between her legs that she wrapped around his waist. She pressed a kiss to his neck, hugging him to her, back to front. "Let me take care of you for a change, hm?"

She soaped the cloth up, sliding it against taut, muscled shoulders. Circle after circle as he sighed, relaxing as she ministered to him.

She wanted to take care of him. Wanted to ease things a bit in a life she knew was hectic and filled with a great deal of responsibility.

"Long as you don't sing to me."

She snorted a laugh. "Are you insulting my lovely singing voice, lawman?"

"Verity Coleman, you are beautiful. You're intelligent. Strong willed. You are eminently capable, you're sexy as sin. You taste like heaven. But you are not a singer."

She giggled, unable to deny his claim. "I had no idea you were out there listening to my rust voiced warbling. It's a flaw, but I keep it within the confines of my bathing tub, after all."

She massaged his muscles as he leaned back into her touch. The outside world was insane. Dangerous. Chaotic even. But right there things were wonderful. Her heart was lighter than it had been in ages.

"Close your eyes." She took up a nearby pitcher and got his hair wet, pouring some of the liquid soap she'd recently come by into her palm and then massaging it into his scalp.

He groaned. "You're mighty good at that."

"I have ulterior motives."

"Thank the heavens for that."

She rinsed his hair and got out to rinse the rest of him appropriately.

He stood and she helped him out, grabbing a towel, drying him. Rubbing over his hair, across his chest and shoulders, down his arms.

He watched her. Quiet. Emotion in his eyes. She got to her knees and finished drying his legs and feet and he pulled her back to hers, returning the favor, buffing her gently with the towel.

"You're the most beautiful thing I've ever seen." He said it so softly it was almost a dream.

She blushed up from her toes. Empty flattery she could take. Dealt with it all the time. But this was something else. He didn't waste words. And it was him. Her lawman. Telling her she was beautiful and that made all the difference in the world.

"Thank you."

He folded the towel and placed it on the side of the tub as it drained. He held a hand out and she took it, allowing him to draw her into her bedroom.

"On the bed. On your belly."

She swallowed hard, but obeyed, her skin hyper aware of his gaze, and then of the cool, slight texture of her bedspread as she lay against it. Her nipples throbbed in time with her thundering heart.

The bed dipped on one side as he got on.

"Close your eyes." He kissed her shoulder. "Let yourself feel."

She did, with a shuddering breath.

"Trust me?"

"Yes." Her answer was immediate. She did. With her life. With her body. With everything she was.

"Good." He licked down her spine, pausing to give a quick nip of her left butt cheek. She giggled at the surprise and then moaned as he nipped again just beneath where her ass met her thigh. And then he licked.

Shivers flew over the surface of her skin. It was delicious and exciting and darkly taboo. His mouth so close to all sorts of places she should be embarrassed about.

He continued down her leg, licking at the back of her knee until she writhed against the mattress. He picked up her foot, kneading against her instep, over her ankle, kissing, nibbling and licking until she was nearly begging him.

But she wanted to know what else he had planned so she bit her bottom lip to keep the words inside.

He dug his thumbs into her heels, up her ankles and calves until she grunted. His touch was deeply sensual, but also reverent. She was glad her eyes were closed against the swell of tears.

So few people touched her in an intimate sense. Not necessarily sexual, but only her sister and Tobin touched her affectionately.

Like she mattered. Like there was nothing else they wanted to do than to touch her, feel her against them.

Loyal had unlocked something she'd buried deep, pretending it didn't matter because she didn't have it and to obsess on it would have killed her.

With him, like this, she was something more than the woman in town who gave you your mail. More than the pretty face at the mercantile or the little lady whose drunken lout of a husband had been murdered.

In Loyal's arms, in this bed, she was worthy of reverence. Worth the time and effort it took to touch her this way.

No one had ever made her feel this way.

Cherished.

He took her seriously. He listened when she spoke. When she talked about wanting to see the rest of the world he didn't chuckle, smug and self-satisfied as he patted her head and told her the big bad world was too much for her pretty little head. He *understood* her curiosity.

The allure of that. Of being understood and valued like that . . . she didn't have words for it. She only knew it filled her up until she was satisfied. Warm and happy and tingly.

His cock pressed against her leg as he leaned over her to knead her arms, as he brushed his fingertips against the sides of her breasts. His beard rasped against her ribs as he kissed her there.

He swept her hair from her back and kissed down her spine again. This time though, he said, "Head down, ass up."

Swallowing hard, her eyes still shut, she obeyed to his hum of pleasure.

His breath against her ass brought hers to a stutter. His fingertips slid against the seam of her pussy.

"When I'm on the road, far away from here, away from your scent and the feel of your skin against mine, I think about you. About how juicy your cunt is, about your taste. I think about the way you're so buttoned up and lovely outside your door, but in here, with me? You're open and eager. You want pleasure, you give it. There's no shame between us."

He spread her, dancing a fingertip round and round her pussy, up against her clit, down around her gate, just inside, and then back against her asshole.

The breath shot from her lips when he did that. Only once before in her life had anyone been back there. It had been done to humiliate her. To break her and bring her pain and domination in all the worst ways.

He paused for a moment, waiting for her to tell him to stop, but he'd asked her to trust him and she would. He wasn't James. Everything they'd done had been totally different.

A brush again, against her asshole and she made herself relax. Again the hum of satisfaction. She smiled though he couldn't see her do it.

Then he knelt, bending and licking her from behind, right up to her asshole, and she squealed. He cracked a hand against her cheek.

"Shh. Keep still."

He went back to it. Licking at her pussy, lapping, fucking into her with his tongue before he pulled back to flick the tip of his tongue against her clit. And then he moved back up again, licking against the rosette of her ass until her spine loosened and she let herself truly feel it.

He bit her cheek again, gently. "Sometimes it's the things we're not supposed to like that feel so good. Hm?"

Starting again, licking, stroking with his tongue until she was on fire for him. Because it didn't matter what he was doing, it felt good, and because it was him, it was all right.

Her slide into climax was slow and delicious and when it hit she breathed through and let it come. She was warm and really wet and ready for whatever he had in mind next.

"I'll be right back." The bed moved and she listened to his footfalls retreat and then return as quickly as he promised.

He got to his knees, looking at the creamy skin of her shoulders, still a little pinked from the flush of her orgasm. Grabbing his cock at the root, he teased her pussy. Sliding in for several quick, deep thrusts and pulling back, brushing the head against her clit until she began to tremble a little.

He wanted all of her.

With a depth of greed that surprised him. Even scared him a little. But he wanted her nonetheless. She gave herself over with ease. Trusted him. It humbled him even as it excited and thrilled him.

He opened the little pot of the cream he used on his skin when the weather was so very dry and he spent long hours in his vehicle. Nothing in it that would harm her or sting. But it slicked things up nicely and it was perfect for what he planned next.

He dug a bit out and, using two fingers, he slicked it over her asshole, and then quested inside, stretching her. She stiffened at the first intrusion, much like she had with his tongue. He'd gathered from the way she froze in certain situations, that her former husband had mistreated her. So he took it slow, giving her plenty of time to see he was different and for her to call a halt to anything she didn't want.

Smooth and very, very tight.

He stroked slow and sure into her pussy, one hand curled around her body to circle her clit gently, enough to keep her feeling good, relaxing as his other hand stretched.

Finally, he pulled out, still wet from her, and began a slow press into that tight rear passage.

She grunted and he petted over her hips. "Push out when I push in. Blow out your breath and if it's too much, say so."

He knew her. Knew how stubborn she was. She'd never say no unless she truly couldn't take it.

He wanted it to be good though. Wanted to show her that everything he did would make her feel pleasure.

"Reach back and play with your clit," he murmured, sweat forming on his brow at how good it felt to be in her. At the pleasure of her submission to what he wanted.

She angled herself, doing as he said. She squeezed around him even tighter once she'd reached her clit, but the tension in her muscles eased a little as she began to stroke.

Another time he'd sit in that far chair and watch as she made herself come. For him and him only.

For the moment though, he was a knife's edge from coming. He wanted her to go first, held on, jaw clenched. "Make yourself come," he gritted out.

She gasped but within moments she thrust back at him as she came, the scent of her body rising, holding him tight and yanking him into climax along with her.

So hard and total he saw nothing but white light as he closed his eyes and let it happen.

Then he pulled out, picked her up and headed back to the bathroom where he washed them both off, caressing her as she looked up at him, a small smile on her lips.

"I think we need to sleep a while." He murmured this as she slid a sleeping gown over her head and then braided the long coil of her hair.

She nodded. "I'll fix you a meal when you have to go back."

He took her hand and they climbed into bed. He was tired. Bone deep exhaustion. But there was something else there. Satisfaction. Happiness. A sense of rightness as he pulled her close, into his embrace, burying his nose in the softness of her skin. And let himself sleep.

BY THE TIME he arrived down at the garrison the sun was rising.

His muscles were warm and he carried a sense that things would actually be all right.

"They're still out there. The ones down on the Highway are still there."

"I think we need to make a move at some point today. We can't just leave them out there indefinitely. They know by this point that you're resourceful. That the walls will protect you. That they can't get over except by that bridge. But that won't last forever. They'll be able to cross when the water goes down."

He and Indigo studied a map for a time.

"Is there a way we can get out where they can't see? Other than the back route the scouts have taken?"

"What do you need?"

He turned to see Verity standing there wearing trousers, her hair in a tidy braid back from her face. But there was no softness in her features. He'd left that Verity when he'd come down here. The woman who spoke now was strong and canny.

"A military trained scout." He shot back her way.

She smiled and he knew he was in trouble.

"I know more about the exits and entrances outside the walls than most everyone here. My grandfather designed the walls." She stepped up to their map.

Indigo snorted a laugh. "Show me, Red."

She grinned. "There's a culvert of sorts here." She pointed. "Tight fit, but you can all get through. There's a stand of trees here that should give you cover."

"And a perch for a sniper?"

She thought for a bit and nodded. "Yes. Many of the trees there are older. High branches are thick. Though you'd have to see how high that goes. At the top they're thinner. Probably could support you, but not if you needed to lay down or stretch out."

"Fine. Show me."

He was an expert sniper. Had specialized training and, in fact, several times each annum he led a training back in Shelter City where he taught a class for the military and lawmen corps.

He hated the idea of taking her out of the walls, but he also realized she lived out there on the Highway and hadn't survived as long as she had by being stupid or taking risks.

"When? Now?"

"Give me a bit. I need to get things dealt with here first. I'll come up to the mercantile to get you when I'm ready."

She nodded, holding up a basket. "I brought some food down. Nothing fancy, but it should get you through the next hours."

Jackson took it with a smile. But his gaze skittered to Loyal for a moment and Loyal knew the other man realized they'd formed a real relationship.

That didn't stop the appreciation in Jackson's gaze, of course. But the man had a sense of honor, Loyal knew. He wouldn't make a move now. Which didn't mean he wouldn't jump at a chance later, if Loyal cocked it up.

She waved and went back out.

"She's one of the best scouts in Silver Cliffs," Jackson said quietly as he ate. "If you're looking to get a sniper's position she's familiar with the geography around, especially given the time of the annum."

"I won't have a lot of time. Once I take out a few they'll take cover so I want to have people at the ready on the sentry posts on the wall in case they try a frontal assault. Indigo, I want you and Marcus in position as well." They'd take sniper positions in more than one spot and take as many down while they had the jump as they could.

And hopefully at the end, the brigands would take whoever was left and get the hell out of there.

CHAPTER ELEVEN

SHE LOOKED up when Loyal came into the mercantile with Indigo and Marcus before turning to Tobin. "I'll be back later. Close up at midday. Go home and check on your mother and brothers."

She grabbed her rifle and strapped it on after tucking the tail of her hair into the back of her dark coat. "Ready?"

Loyal nodded and they all headed outside. "Excuse us a moment," he said to Marcus and Indigo as he guided her away. "I'm agreeing to this on one condition."

She sent him a raised brow. "Is that so, lawman?"

"Yes, that's so. You will listen to me and do exactly what I say when I say it, no questions. You accept my expertise and I'll accept yours. If you can't agree, I'll have someone else show us out."

She snorted. "I'm not slow-witted, Loyal. I am perfectly willing to admit you know things about this that I don't."

"I'm not... I don't think you're slow-witted. I think you're headstrong and you want to help and you might make a mistake in that eagerness to protect your friends and family. I can't if something happened to you I don't know how I'd survive. So do we have an agreement?"

What could she say to that? To that last admission she knew had been difficult for him to have made? Though to have heard it sent a thrill through her.

She nodded. "Yes, we do."

She led them around the garrison and behind the buildings on the main street in town. They skirted the wall, climbing up a sharp outcropping.

"The spot is just ahead. We need to go out single file. There's a copse of trees just outside, and then if you two are looking for other spots, there's another just up the ridge and you can most likely find cover in some of the rocks just south of where we'll come out. Keep low and you should remain out of sight."

"You will come right back through and stay on this side of the wall."

"I'll need to remain here to let you back in. There's a combination on the inner wall that will unlock the mechanism to slide it open."

He sighed, but nodded. He knocked in a certain rhythm. "That's the code. Aye?"

"Aye."

And then she led them outside, sending out a fervent prayer that they all returned safely.

She held the door until they'd all come out and turned. He squeezed her arm but his features were remote, his mind on the task at hand. She did as she promised, heading back to the safety behind the walls.

HE PUT her out of his head. He had to. A series of hand signals to Indigo and Marcus and he made his way up a tree, one that was close enough to the edge of the nearby cliff. He had a perfect view of the brigands' impromptu camp just on the other bank of the river.

They were in closer range that they'd have been at the gates on the wall. Close enough that if he and the others used their shots wisely they could cut that group in half before they had the time to respond. Jackson's men were already in position on the walls at the bridge along with Trinity and Bren. If the remaining brigands made a move to cross that bridge, they'd be cut down.

One way or the other, it would be over.

He heard Marcus' bird song and then Indigo's, signaling they were in position and ready to go.

It all fell away. No fear. No anxiety. Just the job. Each moment fed into the next, over and over.

He breathed out, looking through the scope of his rifle. He centered himself, took aim and squeezed the trigger. Again. Sliding the bolt into place again and taking another shot.

The brigands below fell. Six of them. Loyal took another shot, managing to hit one more as he attempted to take cover. Marcus got another from his position.

Eight down.

Indigo missed a shot and then took out two more.

By the time the brigands had managed to get under cover, the three lawmen had taken out twelve of the brigands and another two or three were wounded.

The remaining brigands shouted, pointing up in their direction. So the lawmen remained still until the brigands shifted their attention to another spot.

When he squeezed back through that narrow slit in the rock wall, Verity was there to open up, her rifle pointed at him until she was sure it wasn't a trick. Smart woman.

"Head back to the mercantile," he told her as she slid the door back into place, bolting it. "We're off to the gates."

She didn't question him, though he could see on her face that she wanted to know. But he didn't have time to explain and they'd be needed so he and the others ran full out to the gates as she turned and headed back to her mercantile.

Once she'd reached the front porch and heard the roar, knew the remaining brigands were charging across the bridge. The horns sounded, announcing a full alert in Silver Cliffs. She ran around back and headed up to her roof, pulling two other rifles along with her as she did.

Tobin was already up there with one of Jackson's men.

She took the field glasses and scanned the gates and the action on the top.

"I think they took out half of the brigands. Maybe more. I counted the shots. I won't assume they made every single one, but given the looks on their faces when they got back inside, they were overwhelmingly successful."

She checked her rifle again and sat, waiting. If they broke through, the rest of Silver Cliffs would rise to the town's defense. She was nervous, but at the same time certain things would be all right.

"Glad the lawmen are here," the garrison soldier said quietly.

She was too.

The chaos didn't last a long time and it wasn't more than an hour or so before the horns sounded again. Lockdown. But they weren't under siege anymore.

The soldier on the roof with them nodded. "I'm off to get news."

She waved, though she remained seated. Once he had gone she looked over to Tobin. "I didn't expect to see you here. I believe I told you to stay at home."

"Father is angry at me. I told him I'd been speaking with the lawmen about their training and would be seeking a position at the academy. He kicked me out as long as I'm *insisting on this foolhardy path.*"

She blew out a breath. Tobin wasn't her son. It would be easier for her to let go than his parents. That was only normal. But he wanted more. And what he wanted to do was good. Honorable. They had three other sons who already worked their farm. Two daughters who would marry and create connections to other families in Silver Cliffs. Her sister would have to let go or lose Tobin entirely. She didn't envy that choice.

"To be fair, I told them you supported my choice."

She winced.

"I'll be hearing about that by nightfall I wager." Her sister would be angry at her for interfering in their family issues. Even if all she'd done was listen and support Tobin's desires. She was the younger sister, the widow. It was Verity who should be seeking their advice and support, not the other way around. That's how Constance would see it.

"I'm sorry."

She patted his shoulder. "Don't be. I *do* support your choice. I hope I can persuade them to do the same. They love you. Worry about you." She understood his position better than he probably knew. She'd had no one when she was younger, she'd be damned if she let a bunch of nonsense keep Tobin from his dreams.

She'd deal with her sister and brother-in-law and hopefully they'd listen to her.

"I know they love me. But I can't just give up what I want. I'm young, it's the time for me to try things. It's not like Silver Cliffs is going anywhere if I change my mind. Can I stay with you? Until things are smoothed over?"

"Of course."

"I'll kip in the blip office. There's a cot in there."

"I have a spare room. Loyal is... he's in with me."

Tobin nodded. "I know. I'll stay downstairs anyway. He'll be leaving soon, I'm sure you'd like the time. And my parents won't be as upset if I'm appearing to suffer on a cot instead of in your house where it's more comfortable."

She snorted a laugh. That was likely true.

"What are you going to do? When it's time for them to leave I mean? I guess they have families. Indigo told me some of the lawmen had wives or husbands, children and the like in the garrisons along the Highway as well as in Shelter City."

"I don't know, to be honest with you. I don't know how I'd feel about being with someone I only saw a few times each annum for just days at a time." And her life was sad, sad, sad that a nineteen-year-old boy was her confidante. "And this isn't just about me wanting him. Though I do. I want to see the world. Be out there. It's not enough to have him show up from time to time. I don't think I'd be satisfied with that."

He nodded. "Have you told Loyal that?"

"Sort of. We haven't even really discussed being together after he leaves this time. It's my assumption we are. There's a connection I know he feels too. He's not stupid. We clearly need a conversation. You know, after we're not under siege."

He laughed, patting her arm.

They watched down the hill. Eyes on the gates and the men and women who walked their tops, lit the sentry fires.

And hoped it was over.

CHAPTER TWELVE

THE HORNS SOUNDED AGAIN after darkness had fallen. They were still to remain on alert, still on a modified lockdown at night with a curfew. But it appeared that the immediate threat had passed.

She went downstairs, leaving Tobin up on the roof to keep watch. Jackson had someone come up and send a blip back to Shelter City. He told Verity they'd killed every last one of the brigands who'd attacked their gates. A scouting party had been sent to the Highway to see if the others had left or were on their way up.

She managed to deal with stragglers to the mercantile. She'd need more supplies soon as there'd been some major hoarding during the lockdown. Though people's pantries would be full, they'd still shop and want fresh goods.

She made some notes for re-orders, and when the traders came to town—and they would after word of the siege got out—she'd be sure to restock from them as well.

The expected visit from Constance came not too long after that. Verity had looked up to see her sister come in wearing a frown.

The place was empty, but she didn't want to have that conversation where anyone could walk in. "Come on upstairs. We'll have some tea and cake while we talk."

She pulled the shutters closed over the windows and doors, her sister helping.

She went upstairs, Constance in her wake.

"I'll put on the kettle. Have a seat." She bustled around, pausing to look out the space in her shutters at the lane leading down to the gates. Still plenty of activity, but not frenzied. Which was hopeful.

"I think the threat has passed. For the time being at the least." She moved to the stove and measured out some tea, spooning it into the pot. "There's some cake there under the cloth if you'd like."

But Constance wasn't in the mood for cake. "I didn't come here for tea and cake."

"Maybe not, but cake is always welcome, isn't it?" She poured the water over the leaves and replaced the lid.

"You're turning my son against his family."

Verity sighed, turning back to her sister who'd moved to sit at the table. Her mouth a flat, angry slash on her normally pretty face. Verity told herself that her sister was upset and to try not to let the digs she knew would come get to her.

"How so?"

"He wants to leave Silver Cliffs. To be one of *them*. I know he got the idea from you. He told us you supported him in this ridiculous scheme. Just because you don't have any of your own children doesn't mean you can take one of mine."

"That's beneath you, Constance. I didn't give him any ideas about being a lawman. He came to me after he had applied to talk about it, to say it was what he wanted. I support that, yes. Not because I'm trying to take him from you. But because I love him. And you."

"You wander around this town like you're a visitor. Always looking for a way out. *Of course* he got the idea from you. If you can't leave, you'll push him away, live through him. I won't let you tear my family apart because you don't have one. Jackson Haldeman would be happy to court you and settle down. If you'd stop opening your legs to the lawman every time he came around."

As a slap, it was a good one. The kind only someone who knows you very well can deliver. "I'm sorry, am I interrupting your plan to keep him here, where he doesn't want to be so you can snuff out any dreams he might have that are beyond your ken?"

"Now who's acting beneath herself?"

"Maybe the sister who just called the other a whore? As for this situation with Tobin? It needs to be said, Constance. He's your boy. I respect that. I'm not putting ideas in his head. Because he's a smart young man. Because he has his own ideas. His own vision of his future. And because you can't punish him for wanting to know what's out there. Do you think you can just tell him no, put him behind a plow and he'll forget?"

"That plow puts food on your table."

"Sure it does. Just like this mercantile puts food on yours. Don't play the martyr game with me. He came to me to share his dreams. Not because he expected me to supply him with more, but because he knew I'd listen and not judge. I'm not his mother. I've never tried to be. I'm his aunt and his friend and I'm glad he has dreams. No matter what they might be. If he wanted to stay here to follow in his father's footsteps I'd be glad of those dreams too. It's not the what of the dreams, it's the fact that he has them. It's beautiful that even out here on the edge he has them. He's perfectly capable of his own wants and desires. He doesn't need me to give them to him."

"You're giving him a place to stay so he can avoid his parents."

"No. I'm letting him stay here until his father cools down and realizes kicking Tobin out of his home because he is afraid for his son's future is an overreaction and a mistake."

"That's not for you to decide."

"You don't get to tell me how to feel or react to anything. I love you and I respect your family. But Tobin is an adult now. He came to me and asked for my help and I'm giving it to him. I urged him to try to patch things up with you. But I won't urge him to stifle his wants for other people."

"Why not? It's dangerous out there!" Constance burst from her seat and began to pace, wringing her hands. "Can't you just tell him that? To wait a few years?"

"The world is dangerous. Shelter City is safer than Silver Cliffs. He'd learn to protect himself even better there. He could very well come back here, you know. He could be a garrison officer if he doesn't want to be a lawman. But if you push him away, what are his reasons to come back?"

"My husband doesn't want me to speak to you any more. He feels you're a bad influence."

That hurt deeply. She licked her lips.

"And what do you think?"

"I think your being unmarried at your age and status is dangerous. It leads the men in town to think things about you that aren't true. But that you won't do your duty for the good of everyone around you makes you, as he says, dangerous. Look at what you've done to my son."

"I already got married for the good of everyone around me. It got me years of beatings. Of rapes and abuse. It got me a drunk more than twice my age. That was for *your* good? Because if that's true, I don't want you in my life either. If you'd wish me back into that hell so your husband or the other men in Silver Cliffs won't want to fuck the widow, you don't deserve me."

Constance, probably for the first time in her whole life, seemed speechless. She stood, her mouth wide until she closed it with a snap.

"My husband doesn't want that. He's a good man. And I didn't know about the beatings. Or any of it."

"Lying is a sin, Constance. Everyone in this town knew. Just like everyone knows Loyal Alsbaugh is in my bed. Like everyone knows

Shawna Parsons is sweet on Susan Anderson but will marry Susan's brother, Matian, instead. She'll bear his children and never act out on her feelings because everyone knows she's wrong for having wants. Right? Everyone in this town knows Floyd Rodders sneaks in Cesna's back door and has at her every time her husband goes off on a hunting trip. Everyone in town knows all sorts of things. I'm done living my life for the comfort of everyone else. Now you need to leave. You've said your piece. I've said mine. Don't push your son away. Let him have his dreams. Let him fail if that's what he needs to do. Have joy at the idea that he may find he loves being a lawman. But let the boy have his own heart. Don't stifle him until that flame he carries inside burns out and he's nothing but a piece of meat with legs shuffling around this town because *everyone* wants him to."

She went to her door and opened it.

Constance licked her lips, but said nothing else before leaving. Verity closed the door in her sister's wake and hoped it wouldn't be the last thing they ever said to one another.

BUT IT DIDN'T MATTER MORE than not being silent. She was done living her life for what everyone else thought was best for *them*. She'd suffered through a marriage far more like a prison sentence. She did her time and now she had moved past it. Oh yes, she knew some of the people in town felt that an unmarried woman in her circumstances was too big a temptation for the married men. As if it was a woman's fault a man couldn't honor his promises to his family.

She did have freedom. More than most. Certainly more than any other unmarried woman in Silver Cliffs. Since her father was dead and she was widowed, she didn't need a male to tell her what to do. Constance's husband had tried. He was a good man, she knew. Only trying to do his best in the world he knew.

But that didn't mean she would show her belly.

Not to anyone.

Never again.

LOYAL CAME BACK to her place exhausted, but glad things seemed to have calmed down at last. He noted the light on in the mercantile and went to check, wondering if an emergency blip had come in.

Instead he found Tobin sitting on a cot in the corner, reading. "

I apologize, I thought Verity was down here. Is everything all right?"

Tobin sighed. "Not really. Can I talk to you?"

Loyal moved into the room fully, sliding into a chair near the blip equipment. "Sure."

"You know I want to attend lawman training. I sent my application in a while back."

Indigo had told him about that. Loyal had approved. They needed young people with the kind of honor and courage Tobin had shown.

Loyal nodded. "He and I talked about that. I may be able to get the fee waived. Each of us, the commanders, can recommend one student per class to attend on scholarship. You'd have to come to Shelter City, pass rigorous physical and mental tests. But if you do, I'm happy to recommend you for that slot."

Tobin's face lit. "You'd do that? Is it because of Verity?"

Loyal snorted. "Boy, you'll find, one of these days, that women can influence your behavior in many ways. But I've watched you grow up over the years I've come here. You're resourceful. Over this time with the brigands outside the gates you've been brave and clever. And you're from out here, from the garrisons. There are plenty of boys and girls from the inner core who attend training. But I think it's important all of the Highway is represented in the lawmen corps."

"My mother said some hateful things to my aunt earlier."

"About?"

"About my plans. Saying Verity put the idea into my head. She didn't. She just listens. She's a good listener. And she said she'd give me the credits. To attend the training I mean. She's letting me stay here. What are your intentions with her?"

"I think that's between me and your aunt. Did your mother bring that into the argument?"

Tobin nodded. "She's headstrong. They say that about her like it's a bad thing. But she's got backbone, my aunt."

Loyal pushed himself to stand. "That she does. I'll speak to her."

Tobin swallowed. "Thank you. For the recommendation I mean. And the advice. She cares about you. A lot. Don't . . . don't ruin it."

He headed around the back of the building and up the stairs to her place. To Verity's small home. She was in her front room, looking out the windows. Smoking a cigarette.

He'd never seen her smoke before.

"How are things?" She asked without turning around.

"Better out there than in here I wager." He moved to her, his front to her back. He took the cigarette from her fingers, drew the smoke into his lungs and gave it back. "Didn't know you smoked."

"I don't. Mostly."

"I hear you had a set to with your sister. That why you're smoking?"

"I want to come with you when you leave."

He paused. "That's what you and your sister argued about?"

"No. Not in so many words."

"Why did you argue then?"

She turned, leaning against the wall, looking him over slowly.

Heat banked in his belly at this Verity. Bolder than usual.

"We argued because Tobin wants to be a lawman. She accused me of trying to steal him from her. Accused me of not getting married and popping out babies for Jackson because I was too busy whoring it up and being a general bad influence on all the good men of Silver Cliffs. I want to come with you when you leave."

"Because your sister is a fluffy-headed idiot?"

"Because I'm in love with you. Because I want to be with you. Because I want to see the world outside Silver Cliffs and I want to do so with you."

"You can't just toss out that you love me because you had a fight with your sister."

She rolled her eyes, her movements dangerous as she stalked past him and into her kitchen. "I'm quite exhausted with people pretending they can tell me what I think or what my motivations are."

"That what you think I'm doing?"

Perceptive eyes looked him over again, dangerously narrowed. His foolish, foolish cock liked it. Liked the air of danger flowing from her, tautening their interaction. He wanted to fuck her so badly his hands shook a little as he fisted them to keep from reaching for her.

"I think I told you several things. First that I wanted to go with you when you left. I've been quite clear since you first came to Silver Cliffs that I have wanted to see the Highway and everything beyond the walls. We talked about it before, though you avoided it at the time. I also told you I loved you. And if you didn't know that, you're a fool."

"Why are you telling me now?"

"You'll be leaving soon. Right? The brigands are gone or you wouldn't be back here. The threat level would still be on lockdown and it's not. Your job is out there. You've been here a week already."

He leaned close, taking her cigarette again and handing it back. One of her eyebrows rose slowly.

"I can't just take someone with me in my escort vehicle. That's not how it works."

"*That's* what you choose to say right now? Do you think I'll wait around for you to flit around from garrison to garrison? Being satisfied with the small bit of you I get?"

"If I said the first thing that came to my mind you'd kick me in the cock."

"And what's that then? I'll give you amnesty. For now."

"That you're dangerous and sexy and you make me want to bend you over this chair, flip your skirt up and shove my cock deep inside your cunt."

"Hm."

He satisfied himself with imagining what she'd feel like when he did get her drawers down and his cock into her. "As for the rest." He scratched his beard. "I may be leaving Silver Cliffs to run my transports, but I'm not leaving you. There are no others I'm flitting to. It's you. I'll be back. For you. Always."

"Which means what?"

He couldn't help his grin and he took a step closer. She gave him a raised brow but didn't move back.

"It means I love you too. Scary woman." He closed the last bit of distance, sliding an arm around her waist. "I'm sorry you had a fight with your sister. I'm sorry she was hurtful. I spoke with Tobin. I said I'd recommend him to the program for a scholarship spot. I can do one student per annum. He deserves the chance."

Her anger lifted and she stubbed out the cigarette, throwing her arms around him. "You did? You will?"

"Yes and yes. It'll be up to him to pass or fail once he gets in, but otherwise, I'm happy to help."

He flicked open the bodice of her dress, drawing a fingertip back and forth over the nipple he exposed.

"You still thinking about kicking me in the cock? Because I'm going to need it in a breath or two."

Her annoyance melted . . . a bit . . . replaced by a smirk. "That so?"

He leaned in, licking up the line of her throat, biting down when he got to a part he liked best.

Her spine relaxed as she gave over to him. Satisfaction roared through his system. *His.* Verity Coleman was his woman and he meant to have her. Again and again.

"You make me want to rut. No one before you has done that to my control."

Her fingers dug into his muscles as she held on. Held on as he licked over her collarbone. She made a sound, a near whimper as he pinched her nipples. Not too hard, but nearly. She arched into him and he let go long enough to back up, spin her.

"Ass out. You'd best hold on to the table. Good thing there's nothing on it."

He bent to pull her skirts up, flipping them to expose her legs. He pulled the drawers down quickly, one handed, as he unbelted his weapons holster and then unbuttoned his trousers, freeing his cock.

"You make me so hard, Verity." He teased her for a moment, his weight against her to keep her in place as he did. Gripping his cock at the root, he teased over her, through slick folds.

So wet and hot. No matter if she'd been angry at him moments before or not. She wanted him as much as he wanted her. A tussle was all right now and again. Especially because his woman was sexy when she was fired up. But he didn't like that she was upset. Didn't like that her sister had said those hurtful things. Didn't like that she'd doubted him for even a moment.

Or that he may have given her a reason to doubt.

"In," she whispered, pressing herself back against him has he teased the fat, blunt head of his cock against that sweet-hot entrance to her pussy.

"Like this?" He pressed in an inch or so, but pulled back.

She groaned and then snarled when he moved away.

He grinned, glad she couldn't see it and get back on her kick Loyal in the cock line of thought.

He wrapped the rope of her braid around his fist, guiding her head to the side, kissing her hard and fast as he thrust into her in one hard movement.

Her gasp of delight was so sweet as he sucked it down, licking over her lips, biting and kissing.

He fucked her as he'd wanted to all day. Deep and hard. Each sound she made, a soft squeal, a guttural moan, he made her feel. He brought from her.

Standing straight, he looked down and watched himself disappear into her body over and over. Loving the carnal way she left him slick and dark. Loving that he was the only man who had this view. That she was his and he hers.

He wasn't ready to come yet though so he changed her angle with his free hand. Grabbing her hip and moving her, canting her hips, staying deep.

She swayed a little though, circling him deep inside. It was his turn to gasp. His turn to nearly lose his mind and groan at how good it was.

That space between him and climax shrank to a razor's edge.

Not ready yet. Not ready to be done.

He pulled out, swallowing her sob of disappointment. He grabbed her, pulling her to the floor with him, laying over her body, kissing her hard, kissing her soft, trailing his lips down her throat.

He loved the way she sighed, utterly satisfied, when he took a long lick of her pussy. Loved the way she slid her fingers through his hair and tugged him closer.

"Get what you want, darlin'," he murmured against her clit.

"Give it to me."

Smiling, he did.

He nibbled, sucked and licked until she writhed beneath him. Until she sucked in a breath and blew out his name on a moan, coming on his lips in a hot rush.

While she was still gasping for breath he got to his knees and pulled her up, turning her body away from his as he lifted her to balance over his lap, arms braced on the floor.

So slick and hot, he slipped back in on a sigh before he bounced her a few times, finding a rhythm he wanted. One she responded to, tightening around him.

Instead of moving himself, he moved her. Bouncing her back against him over and over, drawing close to orgasm slowly but surely. Committing every sensation of her body around his, the way she sounded, her scent, to his memory. He'd be back, as he said. Eagerly. But while he was gone he wanted to call this moment up, remember what waited for him in Silver Cliffs.

When he let himself fall into her, again, that act of homecoming was poignant. Life altering. Beautiful. It grabbed him with sharp claws and didn't let go. Nor did he struggle to be free.

He helped her to stand and noted her smile before he bent to kiss her again.

"I'm hungry. And a little dirty now. What say you let me scrub your back and then I'll make a meal for a change?"

One of her brows slid up. "If you think I'm giving up on the idea of leaving with you because you pleasure me so well, you're a fool," she called on her way to the bathroom. "You can still scrub my back and make supper though."

He sighed, but followed her anyway.

CHAPTER THIRTEEN

SHE'D REACHED HER LIMIT.

Interesting.

After Constance had left, she'd paced the length of her living room until she'd hunted down the cigarettes she'd kept in her kitchen for the rare occasions she wanted to smoke one. She considered a quick belt of some liquor, but she needed to think.

Needed to decide just exactly what she wanted. What she needed and what she could live with.

She wanted Loyal.

She needed him too.

She didn't want to live without him.

So that was the first important thing.

She would continue to support Tobin. He needed that and she wanted it. So her sister would have to live with it.

She wanted out of Silver Cliffs with its too tight expectations on her behavior.

If she stayed, what then? Eventually she'd give in to those expectations. She knew that. It would be harder as each annum passed. As each planting season began, as the snow melted, as harvest came and went, she'd be pressured. And loneliness would be part of that choice. A man like Jackson Haldeman would be a fine husband. More than likely he'd let her have her way in most things. He was nice to look at. Seemed interested in her, but there were other women in Silver Cliffs and she'd eventually have to choose a probable future with a good man over whatever she could have the times Loyal rolled into the garrison for a few stolen days here and there.

Right now it was one thing to live for those times each annum when Loyal and his crew came to Silver Cliffs. But it wasn't enough. She couldn't live with not enough. Not anymore. If she was selfish for wanting it, so be it. But she'd spent several years trying not to fall in love with Loyal and had failed. The last times he'd been in Silver Cliffs, ever since that first kiss, she'd been tumbling head over heels.

It was far too late to regret it. Though she didn't. He was a man worthy of her love. He was exciting and interesting and protective. He was also incredible in bed and seemed to enjoy her company.

He made her feel confident. Like she could tackle any problem. Sexy and smart too. Seeing herself through his eyes had made her everyday life harder in many ways. Made it more difficult to ignore the itch to be gone. The desire to see what was outside.

Tobin had been right that it was time to bring the issue up with Loyal.

But when she had . . . well. He'd gotten all hot and bothered by her attitude. She smiled to herself as she brushed her wet hair out and then twisted it all into a long braid.

He'd gone out to the kitchen to begin their meal after they both cleaned up. He hadn't said much but the way he'd touched her underlined his words of love.

But more needed to be said. She squared her shoulders and headed out.

"Take a seat at the table. I poured you some wine." He worked, chopping herbs as a pan heated on the grill top.

"So they're gone then? The brigands?"

"We sent scouts out to check the ones down on the Highway. Looks like a few escaped from up here and they left. They'll lick their wounds. But you held them off. Not only that, but you're well fortified and you had the guts to blow your own bridges and preemptively attack them. They'll move on to easier targets."

"So you're leaving for sure in the morning then?"

He eased the meat into the skillet, smiling at the sizzle, tossing in some spices before he turned to her.

"Not immediately, but yes tomorrow." He handed her a sliver of fruit. "I *will* be back. The trips will be more frequent for the next season or two."

"It's not enough. I want to be with you all the time."

He opened his mouth but they were interrupted by a knock on the door. He opened it, admitting Indigo and Marcus.

"I'm sorry to interrupt. But you wanted to talk when we got back." Marcus looked to Verity. "Evening, Verity."

She nodded to both men, smiling. Relieved they were all okay. That they'd been in Silver Cliffs when the brigands had chosen to attempt an attack.

"Evening. Come in."

"Thank you." Both men had wonderful manners. Courtly. Indigo had a hat on that he removed immediately upon seeing her. They opened doors and pulled out chairs and, in general, were a delight to be around. Even if they all hadn't been extraordinary specimens of strapping masculine beauty.

They started to fill Loyal in on what they'd seen out on their scouting mission. On the plans they'd gone over with Haldeman for how to deal with the aftermath of the attack.

It went on as Loyal stirred and then his attention wandered. It was clear this was going to take a long time.

She moved into the kitchen and put the food off the grill before it burned.

"There's some fresh bread in the pantry there and some cold, sliced meat and cheese for you all to eat. Milk too, in the cold case. I need to go check on some things downstairs."

Loyal followed her out onto the stairs. "Wait."

"For what? You have a job to do. Just do it."

She knew it was petulant. He *did* have a job to do. But she'd been interrupted so many times it was wearing her temper and she didn't feel like being angry. "It's fine. I meant it. You have a job to do. Come get me when they're gone."

"We'll talk. I promise."

She waved over her shoulder but kept on downstairs.

Tobin came out to help her do a quick inventory so she could finish her orders to send back with the transport. It wasn't as bad as she'd feared. They had plenty of staples left. Flour, sweetener, spices, rice and the like. Building supplies were running low though. Nails and tools needed replacing.

She was hungry so she and Tobin had a meal of bread, cheese and fruit as they chatted about the lawman training he was so excited to start. She tried to avoid the topic of the fight she'd had with Constance, but he knew his mother had come.

"It was unpleasant. But I urged her to speak to you. Urged her to intervene with your father. I repeated my support of your dreams. That's not going to change. I'm sad she's unhappy. I understand, she's worried about your safety. But you want to fly and I'll cheer you on. She and your father will get over it. Maybe not before you leave, you should be ready for that."

"Indigo said a new class starts in a moon."

"Loyal told me he'd recommend you for a scholarship spot. Which will take care of a roof over your head and your meals. I'll send you some credits on a regular basis. You'll have time to see vids and maybe take a girl out to a meal."

"I can't thank you enough. I...it means everything."

"You're nineteen once in your life. That's the time to squire pretty girls to dinner. Or to have a few down the bar with your friends."

His lopsided grin cheered her up.

Loyal came down a while later, just about when she'd started to think seriously on going up and getting in her bed.

"I apologize but I need to go down to the garrison barracks to debrief with Haldeman. It may be a while longer. You should probably go to sleep."

She held back the annoyed sigh, but he saw it in her eyes. He lowered his voice as they moved away from Tobin, Indigo and Marcus.

"I really am sorry. I wanted to have this time with you. But—"

"It's your job. I understand. I do. But this isn't over. You need to know that. We have things to discuss."

He kissed her forehead. "I know. And we will."

She kept his gaze, underlining that. It was time to make a stand for herself. And now that she'd done it, she understood enough to know it had to be backed up.

* * *

SHE'D BEEN asleep when he'd returned to her place many hours later. He could tell, given the folded blanket on the settee, that she'd waited for him.

Guilt stabbed his belly.

That was what her life would be if he took up with her. And he was too greedy for her, too selfish to walk away. He wanted her in a way he hadn't wanted since he'd been very young. She smoothed him out, soothed the rough edges, and he needed her. Needed her like he needed to breathe.

But the idea of her riding along? He'd need to get clearance for such a thing. If he wanted it and he wasn't sure he did. The road was dangerous.

He disrobed in the dark outside her room, moving to join her in bed. They'd need to be up and moving in a few short hours. Back to Shelter City this time to make a report. To get more ammunition and to pack up for more deliveries. He'd teach a class or two, as he usually did when they went back home.

And then he'd start over. Begin a new run on the Highway.

And he'd come back to her. Because he had meant it when he told her earlier. There was no one else for him.

She roused slightly, moving to him as if by instinct. And he guessed it was.

He let her settle, lay her head on his biceps as he tucked her head beneath his chin and breathed her in.

This was something dangerous. The way he felt with her body against his. Not that he planned to do anything else but enjoy it. He liked dangerous things. Lived on that edge all the time. Pretty face, luscious lips, smart eyes that didn't miss a thing, his woman was canny and dangerous, no doubt.

He smiled as he started to drift into sleep. He'd gotten used to this sort of contentment. Oh sure he fell into his job. He loved that too. It was who he was.

But something else was there now, deep inside. Verity had awakened something. A need to belong, a need to cleave himself to something more than his revolver and his vehicle. The badge that marked him as someone worthy.

He saw the same look on Marcus' face when he looked at Trinity. He had liked it because he cared about both deeply. But now he *understood* it.

This was love. Not the thing you said to someone you liked a lot. The kind of thing that was bone deep and inescapable.

CHAPTER FOURTEEN

SHE SMILED when she woke with his arms around her. He'd come back very late. Or very early. Whichever. He'd stripped naked and slid into her bed, making room for her as she'd snuggled back into his body.

His cock pressed at her ass, which was another reason to smile. She could get very, very used to this life. Waking up with a man she loved every day. Waking up with his arms around her, his scent on her skin like a brand.

She managed to turn in his arms. He was awake, she could tell by his breathing. And the smile on his lips.

"Morning." She kissed his chin as his grip tightened.

"Morning, milady."

He filled her with butterflies and joy that floated through her veins like bubbly wine or the need to laugh really hard. And at the same time, he rolled his hips, brushing his cock against her and filling her with other things. Darker things that made her muscles tighten and a moan burst from her lips.

She'd never had this before him. And she didn't want to let it go.

She reached down, grabbing his cock, and squeezed the way she knew he liked. He'd awakened something in her. Well, many some-things. But a sensual thing. She'd wanted before. But the way he desired her had bloomed into something in her belly. An awareness of her sexuality, of the way she affected him. Of how good, how intimate and dark and dirty what she wanted from him was.

And that it was all right because she was his. It wasn't wrong to want him to put his hands all over her in any way he wanted. Because he was her man.

She liked the way that felt when she thought about it.

He rolled her to her back as his eyes opened slowly, focusing on her utterly.

"I want you so much I can't quite think straight. I just had you last night and I want you again. And again."

"Take me." She arched up to nip his bottom lip like he often did to her.

He groaned and followed her back to the pillow, his kiss starting off soft and sweet and deepening as his tongue swept over her lips and into her mouth.

He rolled on top of her, insinuating himself between her thighs so that the notch of her pussy was against the line of his cock. Every small movement sent a shiver through her, another wave of sensation that turned her to liquid inside.

"You're so hot. Wet already. Nipples hard. You want it."

She nodded as he spoke against her mouth. "Yes."

She tried to change her angle by pulling her knees up, bringing him flush to her, slick skin to cock. "In, in, in."

He obliged in one stroke that sent her eyes to the back of her head and her back to an arch.

He grabbed her calves, still kissing her slow and easy, and pushed her knees up, spreading her open impossibly wide. His weight on her kept her in place. Controlled exactly how she moved and when.

She liked it so much it nearly frightened her. But with his hands on her, his weight restraining her, she knew he could be trusted. Trusted to give her what she wanted. To take what he wanted and make it so good she'd ache afterward just thinking about it.

Gasping for breath as he got particularly deep, he nipped her lip, her chin. She cocked her head back to give him access to her neck, knowing he wanted it. Wanting to give it to him if for no other reason.

His beard scratched the sensitive skin of her neck but she didn't care. The burn was good. It sent shivers through her knowing she'd be red from it later.

Knowing others would understand just what made her that way. Maybe she'd wear a scarf. Maybe not.

She smiled at that.

He released her legs and his hands skimmed up her ribs to her breasts, fingers pinching and tugging her nipples until she saw bright flashes of color each time he let go.

"Your cunt tightens around my cock every time I do that."

His voice was rough. Burrs of desire woven through it as he whispered against her skin.

She rocked back and forth against him, pressing her clit to his body, getting just enough friction to drive her slowly, achingly up toward orgasm.

Each breath she dragged into her lungs, each nearly painful bloom of pleasure from the pinch and tug of her nipples, each thrust and drag of her clit against him was like a dance. Just the two of them, body to body saying what words maybe never could.

She knew what he wanted and gave it to him. She gave herself to him freely, understanding he'd demand it, take what he desired and fill her with the sorts of things she'd never dreamed of wanting but now that he'd been in her in nearly every way imaginable, she craved.

"You want to come? Hm?"

She ground herself into him with a little more pressure as she tried to answer but only ended up whimpering a little.

He pushed her legs up even higher, nearly folding her in half. He got to his knees and continued to fuck her. "Give it to yourself. I want to watch you."

Her gaze locked on his face as he watched her hand slide down her belly. The greed in his eyes shocked her as she slid her labia apart and stroked a middle finger over her clit. Lightly at first. But it wouldn't last long. She didn't like it light. She liked it hard.

"Tap it."

He remained there, thrusting as he watched her finger herself.

She lightly tapped her clit, gasping.

"Harder. We both know you want it harder."

Her middle finger came down on her clit harder. Hard enough to make her groan. Hard enough to grab into her with talons and take her a whole lot closer to coming.

"Yes. Like that. Your pussy likes that."

She nodded, stroking with more and more pressure and tapping here and there.

"Wet your fingers. Don't want them to get dry and hurt."

She began to put them in her mouth but changed her mind, sliding them in between his lips. He groaned, sucking on them, the sound seeming to echo down her arm straight to her nipples.

When she moved back to her clit she knew within a few breaths she was going to come and come hard.

"Yes, exactly. Give me one."

Watching him as he watched her was too much and not enough. Stimulating to the point that she wanted to pull it down around her and wrap herself up tight with it.

And she came then, on the third stroke with her slippery fingers. He snarled a curse and then her name. Over and over again as he fucked harder and harder on each stroke until his gaze snapped up to hers and latched on.

He'd never come that hard, or that good. And looking into her eyes as he had tied them together in ways he didn't know how to process much less give words to.

So he didn't. Instead he rolled to the side and she moved close, burying her face in his neck, her arms around his shoulders as he caressed the curves at her hips and down over her ass.

SHE MADE breakfast and they sat in companionable quiet as they sipped tea and ate. He watched the sunrise on her skin.

"Nice to be able to have the shutters up."

He agreed. More because it meant everyone was safe. But the way the light lent her a pretty glow was good too.

"So."

He took a bracing breath.

"I'm sorry about last night. Sorry we got interrupted and that I was back so late."

She nodded. "I expect there was a lot to talk about."

"We wanted to keep an eye on the Highway here and the trails coming up to Silver Cliffs. We didn't want to drive away and leave you open to attack."

"Or get ambushed."

"That either. But it happens. We've been ambushed twice in the last few years. Other crews have as well. I lost one of my men. You're safe here. You won't be out there."

"I understand you're worried. But I don't want to wait around here for those few times each annum you come to town for a few days and leave. I want to be with you. I want a relationship, not a visit."

He groaned inwardly. She was . . . intractable on certain things. He'd seen the steel in her spine more than once, but this was the first time he was sorry for it. He wanted her to obey his wishes. So she'd be safe.

"I can come more often. I told you about the higher frequency of deliveries now. My job isn't only to run transport escorts. I teach at the academy too. We come off the road and have mandated off time every moon. I have a house in Shelter City. You can come stay there with me or I can come here. It'll be more than it is now. But I can't just toss you in my escort vehicle today. That's not how it works. There are regulations about it and even if there weren't I'm not sure it's a good choice for either of us."

"I'm not helpless! I can shoot. I can read maps. Do you imagine I'll sit next to you and ask if we're nearly there every few minutes?" He wisely stifled a laugh at that. "No. That has not even crossed my mind. But I have to be utterly focused on the road when I am on an escort. Not on the beautiful woman next to me and her sweet pussy I'd rather be buried in."

"Are you serious? I can't come with you because you can't think with your head? You trust Marcus and Trinity and I know they have sex!"

"They're trained for the job, Verity. Trinity has been a lawman since she was sixteen. And they're not the leader of the crew. Neither of them. They all look to me to keep them safe. It's my job. I can't just bring my woman on the road with me because she's lonely."

She narrowed her eyes and he held his hands up quickly, recognizing the danger he faced. "I didn't mean it the way it came out."

"How *did* you mean it then? You seem to think I'm asking you to come along, giving up everything here because I'm a sad spinster who wants to be entertained every moment."

"You're not a spinster. That's the first thing. And I don't think, nor did I say you were bored and wanted to be entertained. People try to kill lawmen on the Highway. In the garrisons I have to mete out justice. How will you feel when you watch me shoot someone in the head in the public square?"

"I'd feel bad for you because I know you'd hate it. But it would be necessary and I know that. Probably better than you do. I live out here. I understand the pressures of abiding by the law. I understand lawmen are the line between civilization and brigands."

He scratched his beard, wishing she wasn't so fucking perceptive and undoing all his arguments one by one.

"Damn it. Don't *you* understand what *I'm* saying? I can't bear the thought of anything happening to you. That I'd be the reason for it when you could be here, or in Shelter City, *safe*. I can't risk you out there with me. I can't and I won't. Not because of what I think you'd do, but of what could happen to you."

"I can't stay here. I realized it yesterday when Constance and I were arguing. I will always be . . . beholden here. Stuck in the ways I'm supposed to act. Every day I wake up and I'm alone. And I know it will only be allowed so long and I'll have to make a choice. A choice to marry a man like Jackson or to accept that I'll be unwed and asexual. Right now I'm given some freedom, yes. But my sister voiced something that is totally true. My remaining here without being married will turn people away. So I'd have to turn off my sexuality. No dating. No fucking. Nothing. I'd have to let that part of me dry up so I can remain unwed.

"Or I could just give in and marry a man like Jackson. If I'm lucky. If I don't move on that within an annum or two I'd have less choices. Worse choices. I can't wait for you to come to town the way I have been. Those times are ending. My freedom is drying up. I don't want to dry up and blow away like dust."

He started and stopped a few times trying to find the words. Finally she shook her head.

"You can't know what it's like. You're a man from the center. You don't have to make choices in the same way just to exist. I'm telling you I can't make that choice. I can't. I'm telling you I love you and I want to be with you. I want the world out there, violence and all. Better that than slowly dying."

The horn sounded outside, signaling the start of the day. And the time for him to be readying to leave.

"I *will* be back for you. There's no need to let Jackson in your bed just because you're mad you can't get your way." He said the last angrily and she wanted to throw her teacup at him because he still didn't seem to grasp what she had said totally.

"That's what you think? You think all this is a temper tantrum?"

She noted the wariness in his gaze as he realized the danger in her tone.

"No. I understand your frustration, but I don't like all this talk of other men. Especially when I've told you I loved you and we'd be together. I can't take you in my escort. I already told you. Stay here. Be safe. I'll be back. I swear to you."

She stood up, loving him so much it cut into her belly like knives. "Will you be back to take me permanently or will we have this discussion again?"

"What brought all this on? You haven't done this when I left in the past."

"I'm so tired. I'm done, Loyal. I'm done trying to make due. Being in love with you . . . having you in my bed it's . . . I can't pretend not to see it anymore. I can't be happy living half of a life. Not when I've had glimpses of what I could have otherwise. You woke something up. In my belly. My heart. It's torture to imagine having to go back to my old life when you drive away today. Last night after my sister left I realized I'd been living like a shadow. I had no idea I was capable of loving someone the way I do you. But even for you I can't do it. I'm giving Tobin half my savings so he has credits to live on while he's in training. I'll be stuck here now for several more annum. And I can't be a stop on your Highway map, truly alive for a few days here and there."

"I have to go now. I have to lead the team to get ready to leave." He stood, moving to her, taking her hands. "I love you, Verity Coleman. We can make this work. Please believe that. Believe in me."

She took a deep, shaky breath and pushed past her exhaustion and impatience to remember the feel of his mouth on hers, of the way he touched her. She'd find the patience to wait. For now. "Don't make me wait too long. I love you too."

He pulled her into his arms, hugging her. She tipped her face up and he rained kisses all over it. The tenderness mixing with ferocity and relief.

"I packed already. Will you walk me out?" He took her hand, wanting it to be known that she was his. All the talk about her lack of choices and it possibly driving her to another man had stirred something up inside and he needed to soothe it before he got in that vehicle and was trapped for the next four hours until they got back to Shelter City.

And he wanted to reassure her as well. He knew she remained unsettled. Knew she'd wanted more than he could give just then. But he wanted to give her as much as he possibly could, hating to leave with anything unsettled between them.

He'd never really had concern for much more than his badge and his crew. Something deep had unleashed and flowed into the rest of his consciousness with the sort of completeness that felt like it had been part of him forever. Belonging. He belonged to her. He hated the idea of her unhappiness in a way he couldn't have imagined even just half an annum prior.

Whatever it was, he was old enough to accept it for what it was. It'd be stupid to fight it. He wanted her so he'd take the good and the bad along with it.

"I have to get down to the mercantile anyway. Constance won't be there to help. I've spoke with a few others who work for me off and on through the annum when we get real busy. But there'll be a crush now that the horns have sounded and folks know you're all leaving."

He kissed her again, taking his time.

"I'll be at the escort before you all leave though. I promise."

He kissed her before he grabbed his satchel and they headed out.

. . .

SILVER CLIFFS WAS BUZZING with activity. After the restrictions of the last days and the fear of the brigands, people had places to go and things to do. There was a line up already at the mail window.

And on the porch in front of the mercantile Loyal pulled her close and laid another kiss on her right out in front of god and everyone. It left her breathless and a little weak in the knees.

"I'll see you in a bit then."

She watched him amble away, unable to hide her smile of appreciation.

"He does cut a fine figure going as well as coming," one of the elderly women said as she made her way up the steps heading into the mercantile.

Verity laughed. "Yes, ma'am, he surely does."

She worked a steady shift, taking and bundling mail and packages until she closed up and headed into the store. The crowd had thinned. Tobin nodded toward the door to the loading bay. All the mail was on a rolling cart she needed to get out back. But she wanted to check in with everyone first.

"Been stacking up orders, barter goods and the like near the bay doors."

"Thank you. I'll go be sure it gets on the transport."

She headed through the back and took a moment, standing in the dim behind a tall shelf to find her breath and gather herself.

She hated the fact that he'd be gone again in just a while. Hated that her life would slide back into that place it was before he'd arrived. Worse, she supposed since things had gotten so serious between them. Since she'd delivered an ultimatum and he'd taken it seriously.

If he decided to say no, or came back and tried to push for things to remain as they were, what would she do? She'd use the next break before he came back to really think on her options.

But for right then she'd do her job and also see him off. Store up all the last moments she could before he disappeared like smoke.

When she walked out into the brighter space, she pushed the loading bay doors all the way open and waved at the transport driver. "Ready to load up."

It was quick work from then on. Part of their routine in each garrison. She handed things off and smiled sideways at Loyal when he hopped up beside her and pitched in.

"We're off then. Heading back to Shelter City. Going to do some quick check-ins at the garrisons on the way, make sure everyone is safe."

She nodded, hoping her fear for him didn't show too much.

He pulled her into a hug and she went, squeezing him tight, breathing him in. "Come back to me," she whispered.

"I promise. You stay safe. Keep up the target practice. Stay ready, and if they come and you can't hold them off, you get your pretty butt to that exit in the wall you showed me. In fact, I want you to take some supplies out there. Just store them in the space and if you have to run, you can. Or use the bolt-hole. Either way, be prepared to get out if and when you have to."

That was a very good idea actually. She nodded. "I know the back country well. I can head up into the mountains."

"Good girl." He broke the hug but kept her hand until he jumped down and then grabbed her waist and swung her down next to him, taking her hand again as they walked to his vehicle.

"Safe travels, lawman."

"Safe travels, milady." He slid into the seat and strapped himself in after he'd locked his weapon into the slot on the dash where he could reach it easily in an emergency. His face had lost the softness he'd worn for her and took on the wariness he'd need for the road.

She trailed to the gate as they drove away before she headed back up the hill to the mercantile to work her days through until he returned.

CHAPTER FIFTEEN

AS THEY HIT the Highway back to Shelter City they had a fairly quiet first hour or two. Loyal pushed thoughts of her from his head as he did the job. After a bit it became clear they were riding in the wake of a band of brigands. Whether it was the leftovers from the group that had attempted the siege on Silver Cliffs or not, he didn't know.

"You see this?" he spoke into the headset that connected him to the other vehicles in the escort.

They'd been ambushed before. Caution was a necessary thing out there on the Highway. But they couldn't just drive past without checking for survivors.

Indigo answered. "Yeah. I don't know how far behind them we are."

"The engine on that truck ahead is still smoking. It can't be that far at all," Stace added.

A snarl of vehicles littered the roadside. The tires had been blown, the windows broken. Loyal knew there'd be parts missing from the engines and whatever else could be stripped that the brigands might have needed.

There was no sign that people remained and most likely there wouldn't be. Brigands took slaves or killed everyone. They didn't leave much behind.

"Trinity, Marcus, you two ease up. I'm going to pull over. I want to be sure we don't have survivors."

He got out his field glasses and checked out the treeline. They had heat tech so he could see body signatures, even if they were invisible to the naked eye. Nothing but some small game, which was a good sign there weren't any brigands around.

He flashed his lights and let the rest know what he was going to do, popping the catch on his shotgun and easing from his vehicle.

The men in the transport truck had a mounted gun and once they stopped, everyone was on full alert. Indigo pulled up and got out, giving Loyal coverage.

Burning rubber and metal, blood, the stench of it never failed to clench in his belly. He'd gotten past the wanting to vomit part, but the juxtaposition of blood against the glitter of shattered glass glittering in the sun made a sort of aching, violent beauty.

Blood led him to the bodies. Three adult males with offensive and defensive wounds. So they'd gone down fighting at least.

The central government didn't approve of private traffic on the Highway, but it wasn't prohibited. There would always be people who wanted to do their own thing. He understood that sense of freedom and independence. Sometimes people wanted to holiday down in Shelter City. Or they moved from one garrison to another.

This group though—he looked around—were traders most likely, from the looks of the shells of the vehicles left on the road. Commerce made the world go round.

"Anything?" Indigo approached, his gaze shifting as he remained on watch.

"No. Let's take care of these bodies."

They had powder that would disintegrate the bodies. All lawmen transports carried it. Leaving dead bodies around encouraged disease.

The powder got rid of the attractive and yet deadly target for predators and illness.

It took ten minutes to clean up. Ten minutes to erase the existence of these men, whoever they were. Fathers, husbands, brothers, sons.

A fucking waste.

"Let's go. We got some roadway to make up. Be on the alert, we may roll up on them as they're in action." He turned the engine over and the ferocious rumble slid up his spine. He didn't need to tell them to shoot to kill or anything of the like. They knew what to do. It was always the same.

You couldn't bargain with brigands. Couldn't take them in as prisoners. It was a waste of time and money, of space in the jails. There was one way to deal with brigands and that was to kill them. Period.

They tore up the Highway toward Shelter City. It loomed ahead, shimmering like a dream. If they didn't encounter any trouble, they'd be rolling up to the outer gates in less than an hour.

But of course, ifs were what they were and as they rounded a hairpin curve heading up a steep incline, Bren's voice barked over the comm system.

"Company about a click back."

Shit. They could probably run for it. The brigands would most likely peel away from a chase once they got a little closer to Shelter City where there'd be a higher chance of a patrol and they'd be vastly outnumbered and outgunned.

But they'd have to haul ass with a transport vehicle full of goods.

"Lead them around this corner. If we're clear, get the transport to the rear as we turn to head them off. Vests on. I've just sent a signal to Shelter City operations to let them know we're about to engage the enemy."

Once they'd cleared the turn and there was no sign of an ambush, the transport vehicle, with Indigo and Marcus on either side, pushed past Loyal, who spun his vehicle and got out.

Time seemed to slow down then.

All the training in the world can't prepare a man for this moment. When everything feels slowed down and sped up all at once. When all he'd really have was instinct and hope that his will to survive was greater than his opponent's.

He flipped the holster on his thigh open and chambered a round for the shotgun as he moved to the center of the Highway.

The surface of the roadway beneath his feet vibrated as he took a deep breath to center himself. Indigo and Stace fanned right and left. He knew the transport had pulled all the extra shielding into place and the gunner would have his weapon aimed.

Trinity's footsteps, along with Marcus as they all got into place.

There were no pithy sayings. No hoots or calls to arms.

They all stood and waited until the brigands came around that corner. His muscles burned from the way he held himself until he forced them to relax. This was what he was born to do and he would do it.

Going to one knee, Loyal allowed himself a smile as he aimed and shot out the front right tire and then the left.

The tanklike vehicle lost control and sailed off the Highway into the ravine that ran to the west of the Highway.

"Two more to go."

They came again, around the corner, no slower than the first vehicle.

Bullets peppered the roadway at Loyal's feet as he jerked his attention away from the blacktop to the van barreling toward them.

Still standing, Marcus took aim and shot out the windshield as Trinity took out the driver with a head shot. The last vehicle slammed into the back, sending them both skidding sideways.

Loyal hardened his heart as he pulled a pin and tossed a grenade into the gaping hole the windshield used to occupy.

They turned and went to one knee as the explosion sounded behind them and heat crawled over his back.

He turned again, standing, giving Trinity cover as she and Marcus headed to the next vehicle to finish everyone off.

"No civilians," Trinity said as she came back. "Everyone else neutralized."

But that was too good to be true as shots rained down from above.

"Sniper." They all headed for cover as the gunman on the transport aimed and gave them some time to get safe by shooting into the heavily forested ridge where the shots had come from.

"On it," Stace called out, shouldering his weapon and jogging into the treeline. Marcus followed, his rifle in his hands.

There'd be no more random shooting into the ridge above. They couldn't risk hitting their people. So for many breathless minutes they waited until the sound of a firefight drifted down

As they cruised back through the first ring of gates around Shelter City, Loyal realized it was going to be a longer day than he'd thought.

"Head straight to defense HQ," the guard told Loyal.

The transport went in a different direction but now that they were in the city, they'd be fine. Loyal and his crew headed south, to the sprawling and heavily armed grounds of the defense headquarters.

THE DAYS SLID into a week and then two. Life slipped back into routine. She normally had time with Constance, but her sister had frozen her out. An official blip came for Tobin, saying he'd been selected for the next training sequence and an official transport would collect him. It announced he'd qualified for a scholarship that would cover his room, board and tuition.

It also announced that the next sequence had been delayed by at least two moons because of rising tensions on some parts of the Highway with the brigands. While she was thrilled for Tobin, Verity also knew it would delay the opportunity to see Loyal again. Which had only underlined her position and the need to make a move one way or another when he made his way back to Silver Cliffs once more.

A positive was that despite the blip and his decision to go to Shelter City, Tobin had made peace with his parents and was back living at home instead of sleeping on a cot in her blip office.

But that blip, while not shoving Tobin further from his parents, had been a huge issue between them and Verity.

Despite the differences in their lifestyle and beliefs, Verity and her sister had always made an effort to be part of each other's life. She had dinner with her family at least once a week, babysat the younger boys, took them on hikes and the like.

But her sister's husband seemed to feel Tobin's wanting to go to academy was something Verity had done to them on purpose. A way to harm them and wrest their son from the house.

She'd tried—once—to speak with him about it. He'd been hard faced and angry and had told her she was no longer welcome in his home and to leave his family alone.

To have pushed Constance would have put her sister in a bad place. She didn't want to make her sister's family life harder, even if she was angry. The last thing she wanted was to prove them right and actually work to bring disharmony to their family.

Still, Verity had expected her sister to at the very least try to speak with her about it, but Constance had patently avoided the mercantile and any contact and she felt that absence acutely.

Loyal was gone and things were clearly heating up outside the walls. Instead of the more regular deliveries he'd said to expect, they gotten less official transport with mail and goods and more military patrols passed through.

There wasn't much else to do but work to keep saving credits and to give herself something to do so when she fell into her bed every night she was too exhausted to think about anything.

It hadn't been all bad. She'd hired on extra help at the mercantile.

She couldn't count on her sister anymore and Tobin would be leaving. She hoped to be as well, so it was a necessary thing.

Ruth Hannigan was a little older than Verity was. Married, but no children. Her husband had a herd of sheep and often traded the wool. She loomed beautiful textiles and had helped out on occasion during busy times.

Ruth took to full-time work easily. Learning quickly, working efficiently. They had the beginning of a good friendship already, but the concentrated time together deepened that. Giving Verity a place to go when she'd been rejected by Constance.

Verity found herself at the Hannigan's table several times a week. Sometimes for tea and a chat with Ruth, other times for meals. Jackson Haldeman was their neighbor and he also ended up at the table.

He walked her home from time to time and she liked his company. But he wasn't Loyal. Could she settle with him though? Could she let Jackson court her and be his wife if Loyal didn't bring her an answer she could live with?

Only, she realized, if she could truly make a commitment to him or it wouldn't be fair. She didn't like living half a life, she most surely couldn't ask anyone else to do the same because she pined for a man she couldn't have.

It felt disloyal to even think on that. Disloyal to the man she was in love with. But as Ruth had pointed out reality was reality. She couldn't *not* think about her future in Silver Cliffs if things didn't work out either.

But she kept a firm space between herself and Jackson. A *friends only* space. She didn't want to lead him on or give him false hope. She wanted Loyal. Wanted a chance at a life with him.

They talked about all manner of things, but any time he moved too close to that moat, the place only belonging to Loyal, she gently, but firmly, pushed him back.

She stood on her porch with him after he'd walked her back. They'd had a rousing card game with Ruth and Garner and several other neighbors of different genders and ages.

"Been a while since the lawman came around."

She arched a brow at him. "You've seen the blips too. You know they're busy in the south with the brigands."

"What if he doesn't come back, Verity? Have you given any thought to that?"

She sighed as she moved to sit in one of the chairs. "He promised he'd be back. So he will."

"I know you're in love with him. And I saw how he looked at you. So I believe he'll be back if he can."

The last three words echoed in the near silent evening. The reality of what he did was something she lived with daily.

"If things don't work out with you and him, would you let me come around? Court you?"

She sighed. "I don't want to give you false hope. It's not fair. I love Loyal. I want to be with him."

"I respect that. You're a beautiful woman. Smart and independent. Man'd be lucky to have you at his side, is all I'm saying. I'd like it to be me if things don't work out. I waited, you see. I saw what James did to you. How you suffered. But he never broke you. When he ended up dead and you were free I told myself you weren't ready and I didn't want to push. But then Loyal came around and turned your head at the same time. I waited too long."

"You're a good man. Handsome. Charming. You're not a brute. You have a job, a nice piece of land. There are plenty of feminine glances your way when you walk up and down the hill. There's a woman for you here in Silver Cliffs."

He snorted. "Just so happens she's in love with someone else." His smile was rueful and tenderness flooded her at that admission.

"She is. But that doesn't mean she can't recognize what a catch you are for the right woman. This one? I can only offer you friendship. I like having you in my life. But I can't offer more than that."

He nodded. But she knew how he thought now. Had seen him play cards. Jackson Haldeman was a fan of the long game. He'd made a mistake in waiting, he thought—though he'd been right, she wouldn't have been ready for the first year or two after James' murder—but it wasn't a mistake he'd make again if he got the chance.

"I'll say goodnight then. And we're definitely friends, Verity. You're too good at cards to let that go." He winked, took a step back and faded into the dark.

CHAPTER SIXTEEN

NEARLY A MOON PASSED with no word from Loyal. Planting season had begun in earnest and everyone was busy in Silver Cliffs. They'd had some traders come through so her shelves were stocked, which was always nice.

But that didn't mean she wasn't thinking about Loyal all the time. Wondering how he was. Hoping he and his crew were safe.

Finally, two moons after she'd seen him last, a blip arrived saying an official transport would be arriving within the next moon to collect Tobin to take him to Shelter City to start the next training cycle.

Smiling, she headed out into the store where he stood with Ruth, helping her restock.

"Just got a blip."

He turned, expectant. Grinning, she handed the paper to him. He scanned it quickly and with a whoop he hugged her, dancing around the mercantile.

"I take it we got good news?" Ruth laughed at Tobin's antics.

"I'm going to be heading to training soon." He shook the paper. "Official notice."

Verity laughed. "It's really happening." And she'd be seeing Loyal at long last.

"I need to tell my parents." He sobered a little and her heart ached. She hoped they'd at least feign excitement for him.

"Go on then." She kissed his cheek before pushing him toward the door. "You can have the rest of the day off."

But of course Constance came barreling over shortly after Tobin had left to tell them.

"I can't believe you are still pushing this whole thing after all the trouble you've caused."

Verity looked up from where she'd been counting sacks of grain and then back to Ruth. "I need to step away for a little while. Can you finish this up, please?"

Ruth's gaze cut to Constance and then back to Verity. She nodded and then rolled her eyes. "Yes, of course." Verity nearly laughed but got herself back under control before she faced her sister.

"Let's go upstairs."

She led the way, not looking back over her shoulder to see if Constance was following.

"Now that we don't have an audience would you care to tell me what this is all about?" Verity asked once Constance closed the door.

"You know good and well what this is about. Tobin came running over with the blip about training. This is your doing."

"The last time you were here, I held back because I respected your fear for him. But this is my home and I'm done holding back for anyone. Just so you understand before we continue down this road."

"We just got him back home and now you're filling his head with this again."

"Is that really what you think or are you letting your husband get you all whipped up over something you know Tobin is in charge of?" Anger roiled through her system.

"You're pushing him."

"I'm *supporting* him, not pushing him." She threw her hands up. "Get over it, Constance. Or stop rushing over here to vomit your anxiety on me. You can't have it both ways. If you freeze me out and stop inviting me to family events you can't count on me to let you wring your hands in my parlor and take your abuse. Tobin is a man. He has an opportunity to go and do something he wants to do. You can support him or not, but you know as well as I do that he's going and it has nothing to do with me."

"It surely does. He told us you're helping him with an allowance."

"They're my credits. Mine to spend or save as I see fit. He'll need it."

"And what about you? He *left*. Without you. And you're giving your credits to Tobin so what do you plan on doing?"

Her sister's words, poisonous and full of anger, hit at her like fists, tearing at the walls she'd tried to build around her heart.

"Why are you here? You've already called me names and insulted me. What else is left but to underline it? This is beneath you. You're in my home, you're my sister I'd never try to hurt you this way." She heard the unshed tears in her voice and wished she hadn't.

Constance drew back as if she'd been slapped and then she fell into a chair with a sigh. "I apologize. This tension between us is silly and I'm being a harridan about it. I feel out of control. Scared out of my wits at the idea of losing Tobin. It's been easy to pour all that into my upset over you. I'm afraid for you too. So afraid it's made me angry. I've missed you. I mean that."

"You shut me out. Like I didn't even exist. I've had all this stuff and I haven't had you to talk to about it."

"Please, sit. I'm sorry."

Verity sat next to her sister and Constance took her hands, squeezing them. "I didn't know how to deal with all my fear. And Emeril . . . he's been so angry. I stayed away to placate him. But you're my sister and I was wrong."

Tears shone in Constance's eyes and Verity let it go a little bit.

"Will you tell me? About the lawman. Distract me from the fact that my son will be going off to Shelter City to learn how to be one of them."

"He'll be safe in Shelter City. Safer than he would be here. And they'll teach him to be stronger. You need to keep hold of that when you're scared."

"He's my boy. I know he wants this. I know he'll be good at it. But I'm so frightened for him." Constance swallowed hard. "Enough of that for now. Tell me about Loyal. Please."

"I told him I wanted to come with him. On the road."

Constance gasped, her hand over her mouth. "You did not!"

"I need to be free, Constance. I want to go with him. I can't just wait around for him here. Content to only see him a few times each annum? No. I'd be half a person. I don't want that."

"It's so dangerous out there. How can you want that? For a man you barely know? Explain it to me so I can understand it."

"I don't know if I can. You and I are different." Verity shrugged, searching for the right words. "I can see how it might seem sudden, or that Loyal and I don't know each other very well. But I can tell you that I was married to James for eight years and he didn't know my favorite color much less my birthday. Loyal knows my hopes and dreams. He knows what I like, what my favorite flower is. He brings me books. I know him better than I've known anyone."

How could she explain something that felt so natural? So instinctive it went beyond words?

"I want to be with him. I know others have their wives or husbands with them. Even when they're not lawmen. I did research. It's not dangerous every time. Not more dangerous than being here, only feeling alive when he comes around."

Constance ran a hand over her belly as she thought. "I can't pretend to understand it. How you'd give up the safety of life behind these walls to ride up and down a Highway plagued with brigands."

"If it doesn't work out my heart gets broken. But I can come back here. Or to another garrison. It's not like my life is over. I'll just start another chapter. But if I don't at least try? Now while I can? I'll wonder what if for the rest of my days. I love him. He loves me. It's enough right now."

Constance took a deep breath and Verity knew her sister would never truly understand it. She loved her life in Silver Cliffs. Had never yearned to know things she wasn't told. It didn't make her bad or wrong, it just made them different. But the point would be how her sister reacted right then. Would she revert to anger and fear or would she accept that even if she didn't understand, it was what Verity wanted?

"I can't say that this is a choice I'd make. Or even one I like you making. I worry for you. I can't help it. But I do want you to be happy and I'm sorry, again, that I haven't been very nice about it. It is nice of him to help Tobin. At least he has that on his side."

"Tobin will be with other men and women his age. All wanting to make a difference. From all up and down the Highway. This will be good for him." Pride filled her. She had a very good idea that Loyal was the kind of man that if he had your back others would respect you just for that if nothing else.

"What if Tobin never comes back?"

Verity shook her head. "He will. They get time off. They can choose to staff the garrisons instead of work the Highway too. When that blip came he rushed to you. To share it with you. He loves you so much. He won't be living in your house anymore, but that would have happened anyway. But he'll always be back."

Constance stayed at her table, sharing tea and some cookies. It was the nicest time she'd had with her sister in a very long while and it gave her hope.

I KNOW BETTER than to ask if we're staying the night here." Indigo spoke from where he checked under the hood of his vehicle.

They should. The last nearly three moons he'd been up and down that damnable Highway. Fighting. He'd been shot. Twice. Marcus had taken an arrow to the meat of his thigh and though he'd spent some time in a med facility and the muscles had been repaired, he had a slight limp.

They'd been ambushed. Been bloodied and battered. Had done their fair share of ambushing as well. And bit by bit had retaken the southern leg of the Land's End Highway that had been fairly overrun with brigands who'd managed to take over two garrisons.

Two garrisons where buildings had been destroyed. Where they'd liberated those who'd been tortured. Raped. Some of them anyway. Those who were left alive. The others? There'd been pits where the bodies had been thrown. The central government had to send in the health workers to stop an illness borne from eating human flesh.

The brigands had shifted into something far worse than they'd been before. A new type of band had emerged and there appeared to be some sort of internal battle being waged between this new breed, the flesh eaters, and the brigands they'd dealt with before and were fearsome enough as it was.

They were back to running official transports in the north once more. Exhaustion burned his eyes. But he needed to touch her. Needed to see her. Needed to hear her voice and feel her skin against his.

So yes, they should stay the night in the garrison. But Silver Cliffs was just up the Highway. They'd already stayed two days and it was time to go. He'd done his job and he wanted her so much his skin itched for her.

"The widow Coleman is good for you." Trinity cleaned her weapon at a nearby picnic table. "Being with someone makes you strong when they're worthy." Her gaze cut to Marcus, the corner of her mouth lifting as he turned and caught her looking.

"She wants to be out here with me. And after seeing what we did in the South, I can't. When we left last time it was my plan to make it possible, to get the clearance to have her with me. But now?" He scratched his bearded chin. "I can't bring myself to expose her to that. No matter what she thinks she wants."

He had an alternate suggestion. One he hoped she'd listen to and accept. But there was simply no way he could have her out on the Highway when they could be under attack by fucking cannibals.

He'd walk away before he'd do it. At least if he walked away, she'd be safe in Silver Cliffs behind those impenetrable walls. At least she'd be alive somewhere in the world. He had the stick as well as the carrot. For the time being the military had issued a ban on nonmilitary personnel traveling with lawmen. Even those lawmen who rode along with their husbands and wives had to leave them in a garrison. He'd lead with that before he made his proposition.

"What's the alternative, Loyal? You've seen life out here in the garrisons. Verity wants more. She wants to live outside those walls and she wants to do it with you." Indigo shrugged.

"You know as well as I do about the new restrictions. I have a proposal to make to her about how we can take the next half an annum or so. I guess I'll have to see what she thinks."

"Don't blow it. I've been riding with you for over ten years. I've never seen you do so much as look back over your shoulder when we left a garrison. This woman is the first. The only one you've been drawn back to and that means something." Indigo was far more perceptive than most people imagined.

"It does mean something."

"Let's roll then, shall we? Get to Silver Cliffs. Pick up our passenger for lawman academy. Have an ale at the bar. See Loyal go all cow-eyed at the widow Coleman." Trinity slapped his shoulder and laughed, heading for Marcus, who bent to kiss her before they headed to their vehicles.

They rumbled through the gates and headed back for the Highway. Their pace was harder than normal. He wanted to be there as soon as possible. The Highway was clear. Partially because of the increased military patrols. Partially because they'd beaten the brigands back.

No matter though, because it meant they could get to Silver Cliffs.

The time he'd been away had been torture because he'd missed her, yes. But it had also helped him get to the heart of how he felt about Verity.

Indigo had been right. In all the years of his life, there'd never been anyone who drew him to a place the way she did. Never been a woman who was so impossible to get off his mind.

He was a solitary man. He liked not being owned or having responsibilities to anyone outside the job. His family was his crew, but otherwise no one else held much personal importance to him.

He hadn't been obsessed with fucking before Verity. He got it when he needed to, when he wanted it. When it was offered by a person he knew wouldn't expect anything more than a good time.

But Verity wasn't a woman he could tumble and walk away from. He'd known that when he'd crawled between her thighs the first time. It's one of the reasons he'd tried so hard not to give in to that burning need to touch her. For two annum he'd kept his desire leashed. But each time they'd driven through those gates it had been harder to resist.

Not just the sex, though that part made the blood heat in his veins. So smooth and sweet on the outside but behind closed doors, once they were alone she demanded her pleasure. He'd never really imagined that being as hot as it was. But there was something so deeply alluring in the knowledge that she was dirty but only he saw just how dirty.

She was someone who listened more than she talked. Curious. Vibrant. Full of decency and honor and caring. Verity was a person he could share his future with and it was long past the point where it scared him the way it did the first time he'd kissed her and left Silver Cliffs.

It was what it was. She meant something in his life. The totality of Verity wasn't just her. It was the Verity-and-Loyal of it all. The way she fit in his life, the way he fit in hers. The way the two of them made something else entirely.

He'd held on to that when they'd been out dealing with the death and destruction of the last three moons. He was part of something bigger than his job for the first time in his entire adult life.

And it was good.

CHAPTER SEVENTEEN

THE HORNS SOUNDED and she looked across the store to Ruth.

"Go on and see if it's him. Tobin and I will handle the loading dock doors."

Grinning, Verity patted at her hair. "They have to come up here anyway. And I can see from my parlor better than down at the gates."

Ruth laughed as Verity ran from the store, out the back. The view from her parlor was enough to show her the tail end of an escort heading over the bridge.

Her heart pounded, leaving her slightly breathless, and it wasn't until that very moment that she let herself confront the worry that he'd be hurt out there during this brigand uprising.

She sat in a nearby chair and let herself shake, letting it go so she could gather herself up again, put herself together so she could go back down and greet him.

The procession came up the hill, with the escort vehicles peeling off at the garrison offices.

He'd come when he could.

She smoothed her hands down her trousers and took a deep breath, heading to unlock the mail office. Three moons with no deliveries meant there'd be a lot of work to do.

Ruth's husband, Garner, had shown up to help with the store, closing up so they could get ready for the rush of pre-orders.

With Tobin going she was glad she'd hired on one more person to help, one of Ruth's cousins who ably dealt with the busy times and kept herself working when things slowed down.

She dealt with the sacks of mail showing Ruth just how it worked. It was bittersweet. Tobin had been so great, knew what to do and how to do it. He'd be gone and Ruth would take over. As much as she loved Ruth, as thrilled as Verity was for Tobin, she'd miss the boy a great deal.

New experiences for them all, she supposed as she handed out letters and parcels, checked names off the list and kept the line moving until she looked up to see Loyal standing there, looking tired and thinner than he had the last time she'd see him.

But he was hers and so much joy burst through her it was all she could do to stand there and smile at him. "Well met, lawman."

"I think you need to meet me out back. I have a message for you." He nodded his head solemnly, but the hint of a smile at one corner of her mouth belied the truth of what he was up to.

"I'll be just a moment," she assured Ruth, who waved a hand at her to go.

She forced herself to move at a normal pace until she'd closed the door and then she ran down the hall to the back door and barreled into his arms as he picked her up, twirling her, his mouth taking hers as he set her feet back on the ground.

His taste filled her to near bursting, his arms wrapped tight around her, his smell all around her.

"I missed you so fucking much," he muttered against her mouth. "You taste so good and I'm starving."

She smiled. "You're here."

"I told you I'd come back. I keep my promises."

"There's a mob in the store."

"I know. I have to go back to the garrison offices. I needed to come to you."

She hugged him again. "I needed you to."

"I'll drop my things upstairs."

"I'll see you when we close up."

He kissed her again, his tongue sliding over her lips and into her mouth. She sucked on it and he grunted, his hips jutting forward, holding her so tight she had the mad wish that he'd simply lay her on the grass and fuck her senseless.

"Playing with fire. I'll collect on that promise when I get you alone later." He kissed her one last time, setting her back.

She licked her lips and his pupils swallowed the iris.

"Looking forward to that, lawman."

The rest of her afternoon went by quickly enough. She was rushed off her feet between the mail and the folks coming in to collect their orders. They closed up and spent several hours more restocking the shelves to ready themselves for the next morning when the whole garrison would show up to see what new items had been brought from all up and down the Highway.

Tobin buzzed with excitement. Constance even stopped in with a smile, but didn't work a shift. And that had to be all right. Constance had to make her own choices just as Verity would make hers.

Hers sat in her parlor smoking a cigar, reading a newspaper and looking finer than anyone had a right to. This was often how she found him when he came to Silver Cliffs. But it was different now because he belonged to her.

He looked up at her entrance, stubbing the cigar out and moving to her.

"It was a miracle that I was able to get up here without Tobin in tow.

I sent him off to talk to Indigo. Which was rather mercenary, I know. But I can't find it in me to feel bad."

He pulled her hair from the braid, running his fingers through it, bending to bury his face in it. "Three moons without the scent of you. Sometimes I'd wake up in the middle of the night and smell you, the phantom of your skin. It burned through me."

"You missed me then?" She ran her hands up his arms, loving the warm strength of his muscles. Over his shoulders and downto his chest where she began to unbutton his shirt.

"I did." He put his hands over hers, stilling them. "Not so fast. Aren't you hungry? I'm not going anywhere right now. Don't starve yourself to get something you can have—in abundance—after you've satisfied other hungers first."

"I'm starving for you." And it was true. It had been all day since she'd eaten, but three moons since he'd touched her. Since she'd had her hands on him, heard his voice.

"I made dinner." He put her in a chair. "Sit and let me take care of you. Then I'll take care of you some more."

He sauntered into her kitchen, pulling something from the oven that smelled very good, before dishing some onto two plates that he brought to the table. "I saw the bread, it's there under the cloth. I brought some butter as well. It's got salt from the Great Sea. I think you'll like it."

He bent to kiss her temple. "Don't pout or I'll give you something to do with that mouth besides eating."

Her gaze locked with his and she breathed in deep, letting what he did to her settle into her bones. So good. He woke up every bit of her senses. All her wants. Just looking at him made her ache.

It was a delicious sort of ache though. She licked her lips, loving the way his breath hitched.

"Promise?"

She watched, her nipples hardening, as he reached for his belt buckle and undid it, sliding his trousers open and pulling out his cock. Everything inside her stood up and cheered at the sight.

"Go on then." He tapped the head of his cock, wet with precome, against her lips. But she opened, licking across, tasting salt and skin and Loyal. She hummed her satisfaction at that.

He hissed and she took the head to the crown into her mouth with a swirl of her tongue.

"Yes."

She fought against the lure of closing her eyes and sinking into the sensation that way. She didn't want to miss the sight of him. Of the way he gazed down his body at her. Hungry.

Little by little she swallowed more of him. Taking him deeper and then deeper again. Finding her pace, getting her breath just right. His taste didn't flood through her, instead she absorbed it in increments until, before she fully realized it, he owned her.

He smoothed a hand down her hair, brushing her jawline, her cheek, the side of her mouth.

"So beautiful. There's so much ugliness out there and then there's you. You who washes it all away every time you touch me."

She moaned around the cock in her mouth. She tried to tell herself she'd be tough when she gave him her ultimatum, but how could she resist him? In the flesh as he said things like that with the truth of it written all over his face? She wanted him and she wanted things to work.

But for that exact moment she wanted to bring him pleasure. So she focused, licking up the line of him, delighting in his rough moan, of the way his hand had moved back to her hair to gather it, to move her at whatever pace he wanted.

"You want it in your mouth? Hm?"

She nodded.

His curse delighted her. Just a small slip, a tiny chink in his control. And she did it.

His hand tightened, her scalp tingled as the pain slid into something else, as the taste of him filled her, as his tortured groan was homecoming.

He had a plan, damn it. He'd make her a meal, strip her naked, bathe her, eat her pussy a few times, fuck her boneless and then they'd talk. But she was temptation personified. So lovely. Beautiful and sweet and soft but just beneath that softness there was an edge that drove him to possess her, to cosset and protect and take. Take and take.

He bent to kiss her, shaking his head at her satisfied smile.

"Welcome back, lawman. Now where's my dinner?"

"Can you wait then? For me to sate other appetites?"

She laughed, sipping the ale he'd poured. "I can wait. I know you'll make it worth it."

She buttered some bread and dug into the casserole he'd made, sighing happily. "In addition to everything else you're good at, you can cook. I'm not quite sure how you haven't been snapped up before now."

"Never wanted to be. Until now."

He took her hand after he sat. Squeezing it before digging in. "So fill me in on what's happened over the last three moons."

She waved it away. "You have a much better story I'd wager."

"Not while we're eating. It's not a story that goes well with food. I see you have new staff in the mercantile."

"That's Ruth. She's going to take over when Tobin leaves. She's wonderful and a fast learner. I think she's better at running things than I am. Endlessly patient. A good friend too. Tobin is"—she shook her head, amused—"so excited. He fair bounces around town all day long. Any time the horns go off he runs to see if it's an official transport to pick him up. Jackson has been helping him with target practice and tracking. Most folks are proud to see him go and represent us down in Shelter City."

Most. "So you're still having trouble with your sister then?"

She told him about how they'd stopped inviting her over, about the things her sister had said. And about their recent attempt to patch things up in some way.

"I'm sorry I've brought you heartache."

"It's not that. It's . . . I think it's that I'm different now. I want different things and while most folks in Silver Cliffs are all right with that, some, like Constance and her husband, they're not. They're so frightened by whatever is outside the walls that my wanting to see it is threatening somehow. I don't know. But what can I do? Give up on what I want to make them comfortable? Why should I do that?"

They skirted around it, the gauntlet she'd tossed down when he'd left the last time. It was cowardly to avoid it, but he'd wanted a bubble. Just the two of them, no stress. Even for a brief time.

She smirked. "Just because we're not talking about it doesn't mean we're not thinking about it."

"How do you do that? Know what I'm thinking?"

She laughed, putting her head on his shoulder a moment. "It'll be our secret that you're really not so mysterious."

"Let's eat first. Then can we get naked and in your lovely tub? We'll talk. I promise. But let me have you, soak you up for a bit." He needed that more than he'd realized until right then.

"All right. The doors are locked so as long as we aren't beset by brigands or Tobin, we have time."

They talked of nothing too serious. She told him what she'd been up to. Training Ruth, making a new friendship. She skirted around her interactions with Haldeman, which amused him more than angered him. He had no worries about her constancy. The man *was* a threat, but not an immediate one.

"I'll clear the dishes if you'll run the bath?" He took her hand, turning it and kissing the heart of her palm. She shivered and he smiled.

"You're a rogue. I rather like it."

What he liked was the breathless way she spoke.

"Only for you. All for you." He pulled her close, swaying. She made him feel things he'd never understood. Had seen, knew existed between others, but had never begun to feel.

"You make me want things, Verity." He brushed a kiss against her forehead, pushing her hair back to expose more skin. More to touch.

"I'm glad I'm not alone."

He breathed her in deep. Needing that. She chased away the stench of death. Of misery and pain. Filtered it all out and left him better.

"I'll go run the bath."

"I brought you some candles and a few other baubles you might like."

She tipped her head back with a smile. "You did?"

He nodded. "I'll be in momentarily."

She tried not to rush as she lit the candles he'd brought. The scent of them filled her bathroom, casting a golden glow on the walls. The same walls she'd seen every day for so long. They'd been a different color when she lived here with James. But after he'd died she repainted. Changed things to suit herself and chase his energy away.

She disrobed, letting her hair stay free, knowing he liked it best that way. Several bundles sat on the bed. She unwrapped the red one first, finding earrings of deep blue glass. She smiled. No one gave her presents, not the way he did. Not always practical, but fun and pretty.

She replaced her other earrings with the blue ones and then opened the next. A scarf. She drew it over her skin. So soft.

"I thought it would look beautiful against your skin and I was right."

She turned to find him standing there, naked. She sighed happily. "You're the best present of all."

"I turned the water off."

She brushed her hair back to show him the earrings. "They're lovely, thank you."

"I have a confession to make."

"And what's that then?"

"My home in Shelter City is full of presents I've picked up for you over the years. I didn't want to scare you with how often you came into my thoughts. So I have them tucked in drawers and on shelves. I tell myself I'll give them to you bit by bit, but I keep finding new things that call to me. The scarf I picked up at a bazaar after the first time I came here."

She swallowed past a lump of emotion. "I don't know what to say that could do justice to how much that touches me."

"You were so lovely the first time I saw you." He took her hand and drew her into the bathroom. "We drove up that hill and I liked Silver Cliffs immediately. Well defended. Which makes my job easier of course."

She got in the tub and he settled in behind her, pulling her against him. Where she belonged. "It was the middle of the warm season. You came here and people were chattering because our old escort had retired. You got out of the lead vehicle and I just watched you."

"Yes. It was warm. You came out of the loading bay, your legs showing in a flowy dress. Pale blue. You had shadows in your eyes, but you smiled at me. I wanted you then. But you weren't ready."

She really was fortunate in the men who fancied her. Both Loyal and Jackson had said the same thing. Had given her time and space to find her feet in the time after James was killed.

"You weren't ready and neither was I. I suppose the more I got to know you, the more I understood that too." Their fingers tangled as they held hands. "I knew, deep down, that you were not the kind of woman I'd be able to walk away from. And once I took a taste." He paused to laugh. "Once you demanded I did and I finally let myself, there was no turning back. It's not just that I'm in love with you. It's that I cannot imagine a life without you. I need you."

Tears pricked against her lashes. The man barely said ten words in a row and there he was, making this most moving declaration of love.

"I don't know how I ended up with you. You're a miracle. My miracle and I cannot let you drive with me. Not right now."

Her heart got stuck in her throat and she forced herself to be calm, to listen to all he had to say and she hoped it would be enough.

"There's a schism in the brigand leadership. The ones we faced over the last three moon " He held her tighter and she shivered at whatever could make a man like him speak with that tone of fear and horror. "They're cannibals. Not just the sharpened teeth to tear into foes when they attack. That's part theater, part weapon. But these new ones." He swallowed. "There's a new illness in some of the garrisons they overran. A virus that comes from eating human flesh. They are I can't risk you. It's one thing to risk you when you can handle a weapon and would be riding along with my crew, who are all highly skilled. But they had mass graves. The women and children had been defiled in unspeakable ways. I've seen a lot, but this was . . . I've never seen anything like it. I tell you this level of detail because I want you to understand that when I came to the last few miles until the first gates of Shelter City when I left you last it was my plan to seek permission to have you ride with me."

Chills ran across her arms and he held her closer. "I can't protect you from that level of depravity. And the central government has issued a temporary ban on nonmilitary personnel riding along so it's not just me."

"So what do we do then?"

"It's a good sign you're not slapping me, I guess."

She snorted. "I want to be with you. But I'm not thick. I know this is bad. I know you have your reasons and they're good. I don't want to get tortured, raped and eaten for dinner by brigands any more than you want to."

"We get time off. I've arranged for some. I have this run to make but we'll be back to get Tobin and head to Shelter City. Would you like to come with me? Stay with me a while? I can show you around. We can have every day with each other. And, if you like Shelter City and my home, well, you could be my wife and live there. Or here. Once things get better you can ride along. But in Shelter City you can take classes, see vids, stand in the big sea. Be in my bed. I'm in Shelter City more than I can be here. But we can make it work. Whatever you want, if I can give it to you, I will."

She got to her knees and turned to face him. "Did you just ask me to marry you?"

He nodded, not speaking.

CHAPTER EIGHTEEN

DRIVEN TO SEE HER, he got out of the vehicle and nodded at Indigo. "Short of bleeding or something being on fire, if anyone disturbs me and my wife in the next two days or so, I will cut someone."

Indigo laughed. "Understood. Tell Verity I said hello and will see her when you're ready to unchain her from your bed."

Hm, that sounded like something he should try.

He waved and turned back to the house. A place that had been just somewhere he slept in between runs. For years. But now it was a home.

Dawn crept over the horizon as he let himself inside, heading to her. Always on his way to her.

She slept in their bed, a tousle of hair around her face, the blankets wrapped around her. A book lay open on the bedside table. One of the books from a class she was taking at the university.

She'd thrown herself into life in Shelter City with wild abandon. While he was away, she took day trips to some of the temples on the outskirts of Shelter City. She learned to swim in the ocean. Spent time with Tobin, who was thriving in his training. She'd made friends there as well. Neighbors, mostly, but people from her classes, some of the spouses and partners of the lawmen they knew as well.

They'd gotten married, just the two of them along with the officiant, on the sand with the roar of the big sea as their music. She was the heart of him. Vibrant and beautiful. Filling his life with music and love and so much desire his skin was tight with it. She opened her eyes as she shifted to her back. "I heard you come in. What are you standing all the way over there for? It's been some time since I've been pleasured by anyone but myself."

He forgot everything else but her as he yanked his clothes off, sending things flying as he moved to her. Always to her.

Her skin was warm, fragrant with the soap she used, her hair soft, thick and cool against his arms as he got in bed, pulling her to him, kissing her hard and long. Taking all she offered so freely.

Two quick movements and he'd tossed away the nightgown she wore and her drawers, leaving her bare and eager.

"Your own hands though? Busy?"

"It helps me sleep." She arched as he kissed her neck. "Not nearly as well when it's your mouth or hands instead of my fingers, of course. I'm sure you're forced to make do with your hand while you're gone too. Especially as your wife"—she paused to growl when he found her nipple and licked over it—"mmm, would shoot your cock off if you put it anywhere near another woman."

"It's a sign of just how messed up I am, my love, that it gets me hot when you speak like that."

She laughed, squirming as he dragged his teeth over her nipple and sighed as he kissed down her ribs, dropping to her belly button and down, pushing her thighs open wide and breathing her in.

Hunger for her dug in deep as he slid her labia apart with his thumbs. He licked her over and over, taking her taste into himself until his restlessness, the restlessness that came from being away from her, eased.

She slid her fingers through his hair, tugging him closer, her hips moving back and forth against his mouth. Taking her pleasure.

It lit him up. Made him so hard he ached as his cock pressed into the blankets beneath where he lay. His face buried in her cunt so that he was surrounded by her. His tongue dug up into her, mimicking what he'd be doing with his prick shortly.

She made one of her sounds, a pleading sort of moan. He knew she was close. So wet against his lips, her thigh muscles trembling where he held her apart with his shoulders.

When she let go, she grabbed her pleasure up and wallowed in it. Trusting that there'd always be more when he was involved.

He'd been gone two weeks, which was better than three moons, to be sure. And when he stayed it was in their home. She woke up with him every day. He took her to breakfast or out to the ocean.

Her ring glinted on her hand as he surged up to kiss her. She wrapped her arms around him and her thighs, just as he slid into her body and she arched to get him deeper.

He didn't hurry. Just the slow advance and retreat. Filling her body over and over until she warmed up and accepted that he was home. She dug her nails into his ass, urging him on. "More. Deeper, harder. More."

"Greedy." He kissed her again, the scruff of his beard tickling her lips.

"Always. For you, always."

"I'm a lucky husband that way." He kissed down her neck, changing his angle, hitching her hips up and giving her what she'd asked for. Harder. So hard her tits bounced as waves of pleasure shot through her with each thrust.

"Mine," he whispered.

"Yes."

"I surely do love you, Verity Alsbaugh."

"Thank you, lawman. I love you too."

She laughed as he came. Filling her up with joy and the wonder of connection that seemed to grow stronger each day.

He snuggled back down to the bed, remaining half inside her. "I'm home."

"Mmmm. Welcome back."

SIGN UP FOR LAUREN'S NEWSLETTER

Don't want to miss Lauren Dane's latest book? Sign up for Lauren's newsletter and get notified when she has a new one out.

www.laurendane.com/newsletter

COMING UNDONE

INSIDE OUT

NEVER ENOUGH

LAID OPEN

DRAWN TOGETHER

CASCADIA WOLVES

Paranormal Romance

RELUCTANT MATE (formerly *Reluctant*)

PACK ENFORCER (formerly *Enforcer*)

WOLVES' TRIAD (formerly *Tri Mates*)

WOLF UNBOUND

ALPHA'S CHALLENGE (formerly Standoff)

BONDED PAIR (formerly *Fated*)

TWICE BITTEN (formerly *Unconditional*)

CHASE BROTHERS

Contemporary Romance

GIVING CHASE

TAKING CHASE

DELICIOUS

Contemporary Romance

SWAY

TART

LUSH

DIABLO LAKE

Paranormal Romance

MOONSTRUCK

PROTECTED

AWAKENED

FEDERATION CHRONICLES / PHANTOM CORPS

Sci-Fi/Futuristic Romance

UNDERCOVER

RELENTLESS

Phantom Corps:

INSATIABLE

MESMERIZED

CAPTIVATED

GODDESS WITH A BLADE

Urban Fantasy

GODDESS WITH A BLADE

BLADE TO THE KEEP

BLADE ON THE HUNT

AT BLADE'S EDGE

WRATH OF THE GODDESS

BLOOD AND BLADE

GODDESS WITH A BLADE VOL. 1

GODDESS WITH A BLADE VOL. 2

HURLEY BOYS

Contemporary Romance

THE BEST KIND OF TROUBLE

BROKEN OPEN

BACK TO YOU

INK AND CHROME

Contemporary Romance

OPENING UP

FALLING UNDER

COMING BACK

METAMORPHOSIS SERIES

Sci-Fi/Futuristic Dystopian Romance

ALL THAT REMAINS

ALL THE LITTLE PIECES (*coming soon*)

PETAL, GEORGIA

Contemporary Romance

ONCE AND AGAIN

LOST IN YOU

COUNT ON ME

ABOUT LAUREN DANE

The story goes like this: While on pregnancy bed rest, Lauren Dane had plenty of down time so her husband took her comments about "giving that writing thing a serious go" to heart and brought home a secondhand laptop. She wrote her first book on it before it gave up the ghost. Even better, she sold that book and never looked back.

Today Lauren is a *New York Times* and *USA Today* bestselling author of over sixty novels and novellas across several genres.

For more information:
www.laurendane.com